A Stone Heart For Christmas

MADDIE DANIELS

Contents

Chapter One

As I heaved the near-bursting garbage bags into the dumpster, I thought for the umpteenth time about how I should have been spending my Winter holiday season: on a beach, sipping cocktails with my fiancé, Johnathan. Except, he was my ex-fiancé now. I was still getting used to that.

Instead, I was taking out the trash at the cafe where I worked, while getting verbally harassed by suburban mothers who were feral for limited edition coffee mugs and Hazelnut caramel lattes. I had picked up more shifts after Johnathan had broken up with me in September. All of this happened right as we were planning our Christmas vacation to Tulum, Mexico.

As I trudged back inside, shivering from the cold, I tried not to think about how he had used our wedding planning as the factor that drove us apart. How he claimed it was all too stressful, to the point where he wasn't sure what he wanted anymore. Of course, what he really meant was that he wasn't sure what he wanted with me anymore. He strung me along until one day when he went to take a shower and accidentally left his phone on the couch, usually he brought it with him everywhere. It buzzed and I curiously snuck a peek at the notification. It was a text from a woman he worked with, claiming she missed her "Johnny" so much. I had confronted him about it and we fought until he confessed: he had cheated on me with another woman and had feelings for her. I was crushed by this. I expected him to apologize, to tell me he would make it up to me somehow. I was so hurt but I still wanted to fight for us. I wanted to forgive him. We were supposed to get married in the Spring. Instead, he made no excuses, he simply broke off our engagement and moved out. I sold the engagement ring because it hurt too much to look at. I blinked back stupid tears that threatened to fall and wiped my eyes with the sleeve of my white barista blouse.

I looked at the line of impatient customers, chatting loudly, eager for a coffee or a frappe, not a care in the world except their sweet treats for a day of shopping at the outlets. Admittedly, I wanted to be them. I wanted to be anyone else right now. But life had dealt me a different hand. I straightened my apron and got to work.

"Hey Erica! Mind covering the register for me for a few minutes?" Jennifer implored with a pleading look, pouting cutely as if that would affect me.

"I'm not on the register today, Jenn," I reminded her evenly and continued to work on the drink in front of me. Normally, I was always ready and willing to help out my coworkers, but Jennifer had a habit of abandoning her post and leaving everyone else to pick up her slack. For once, I was over it.

"Please! I really have to use the bathroom." Instead of waiting for confirmation, Jennifer turned toward her waiting customer, nodded in my direction, and said, "She'll be right with you," before dashing off, blond pony-tail swinging in her wake.

Wow. I rolled my eyes, irritated. *Jenn was really something else.* How our boss had never once reprimanded her for her behavior, in all the time we had worked togeth-er was beyond me. I figured it was nepotism. Her uncle owned a location of Brewed Luxe, a few towns over, after all.

I took my time finishing the latte I was constructing. It wasn't the waiting customer's fault, but I didn't want to just dash over when called like an obedient dog.

I placed the finished latte on the counter. "Carol!" I called, and watched as a young woman carrying a bookbag took her drink. Then, begrudgingly, I ambled over to the register to assist Jennifer's customer.

"What can I get for you?" I asked curtly, not looking up at them.

"That was pretty rude of Jennifer to dump me on you," came the customer's velvety, deep voice.

I raised my head at the customer's unexpected comment, and when our eyes locked, my stomach flipped in midair. This guy was what I could only describe as breath-taking and "expensive-looking." In short, the guy looked like he walked off the set of a television show. He stood at least six feet tall, and was well-built, with thick dark curls that framed his sculpted cheekbones. He wore a gray designer cashmere trench coat over a black dress shirt and tailored pants. He was smiling right at me, holding me in place with those brilliant gray eyes that complemented his smooth, olive complexion. I exhaled, my heart racing like a gazelle.

"I-It's no problem," I stammered, tucking a few of my box braids behind my ear, suddenly finding it difficult to maintain eye contact. "Er, what can I get for you?"

"Cortado large, please."

"Coming right up." Miraculously, Jennifer was back from the bathroom in a decent amount of time. Still, I gave her a pointed look and went to make the customer's drink while she took his payment.

"You didn't ask for my name," the customer said, following me down the length of the bar as I started on his beverage.

That's because I got lost in your eyes, dumbass. I obviously did not say this out loud.

"What is it then?" I asked, conceding.

"Devin."

I nodded and wrote it down on his cup, not trusting myself to say much. Why I was suddenly feeling nervous was beyond me. I wasn't usually like this. Plus, it wasn't like he was the first handsome guy to walk in here. So then, why did this feel so different?

"And yours?" he queried sweetly, voice breaking through my anxious thoughts.

I took him in, noting the way he looked at me, smiling a little, his gaze playful. He was obviously flirting. He was hot, but I didn't have time for this. I was too sad about Johnathan and too stressed to flirt back.

"I don't think that's necessary," I said nonchalantly, handing him his drink. As I reached out to place it in his hands, he encircled my wrist with his warm palm and held it. I stiffened and looked at him. His head was tilted innocently, like a puppy dog, I thought absently, as his eyes beseeched mine for an answer.

For whatever reason, I didn't fight it anymore. I sighed in mild annoyance, "it's Erica."

A gentle smile spread across his lips, and he released my hand. "Erica. Thanks for the drink." He turned away, taking a napkin from the dispenser with him.

As if in a trance, I watched him leave, unable to shake the feeling in my bones.

"*Damn* girl," Stevie, my favorite workplace friend, giggled and nudged me as she passed. "He was *hot!*"

"He *grabbed* my wrist when I handed him his drink," I said, still reeling from the experience.

"Like I said, *hot*." Stevie did not see a problem with this. "Man's got rizz, Erica."

"Rizz?" I repeated, bemused, my face scrunched up in confusion.

"Yeah," said Stevie, turning back to look at me like I was an alien. "Short for charisma? Come on, I know you're middle-aged, but even you should know that one."

I scowled at her. "Ok, first off, twenty-eight is far from middle-aged. Secondly, normal people don't take internet slang offline. And thirdly, grabbing a stranger's hand constitutes as kinda creepy."

Stevie, being her good-natured, perky self, just laughed. "I like guys who aren't afraid to show interest in what they want. Real dom energy."

I shook my head at Stevie's one-track-mindedness, smiling despite myself as I started on the wave of new orders that had begun to pile up since Jennifer's return to the register.

"He was totally flirting, Erica!" Stevie insisted, refusing to let up. "You should have went for him."

"No thanks," I dismissed the idea immediately. "I just got dumped while planning my wedding, in case you forgot. I can't even see myself with someone new already. Give me one to two years to mourn at least."

"Girl, there's nothing like a good fuck to ease the breakup pain. That's what I always say," Stevie said before bustling past me with food for drive-thru window.

I pinched the bridge of my nose in mild annoyance. Stevie spoke from experience: she hooked up with anyone she found attractive and wanted. I had never been one to have sex on the first date, and one-night stands were completely out of the question. Although Jonathan wasn't technically my first real boyfriend, I had shared a lot of my firsts with him. And, that's partially why I had cherished our relationship so much. He had shared a lot of his firsts with me as well. At one point, he had been so excited to spend our lives together. He had once told me we were endgame. Yet, he called off our wedding plans, and dump me just a few months later for a chick at his office.

In this moment, I envied the ease that people like Stevie seemed to have with non-committal, carefree relationships. Stevie used men for whatever she pleased, including entertainment and companionship, dinners, vacations, shopping sprees, paid bills, and sex. Then, when she got bored or the guys got "attached" or became "annoying," she'd simply move on. More than once, the girls at work had asked Stevie to teach them her ways. She always joked she'd write a tell-all book.

Before I knew it, my shift had finally ended, and I was in my car on my way home. The sun had fully succumbed to the darkness of night, but all I felt was a blanket of anxiety cloaking me in its emptiness. It happened often these days, especially since Johnathan and I separated. One thing people hardly discuss is the grief that broken relationships create, not only for the person but for the life you had pictured together.

One moment, I was living my dream; the next moment, it was gone, and I was hit with my cold, empty reality. I scolded myself; I should have known better than to feel too happy. Life has a way of reminding you how cruel and unpredictable it was.

I felt my lips quiver, and willed myself to get a grip, clutching the steering wheel as if it would help to anchor me in reality. As I turned on my street, I took a deep breath, mentally preparing myself to enter a lonely home where Jonathan's absence now lingered in every corner.

Taking my purse, I stepped out of my car. The moonlight illuminated my path to my front door. Suddenly, a rustle in the nearby bushes made me jump and whip around in fright. I'll never forget what I saw. I could only describe it as a pair of glowing yellow eyes staring back at me from within the darkness. A chill ran down my spine as I felt fear rising within me. It was as though I was paralyzed, rooted to the ground, all while time seemed to stand still. Finally, I snapped out of it and mustered up enough courage to sprint towards the safety of my home. As soon as I made it inside, I slammed the door shut and locked it.

I slid down the door, gripping the fabric of my jacket over my pounding chest, and sighed in relief.

What the hell was that? I must be going crazy...

Chapter Two

Devin

It could have gone better today, I thought from my place in the bushes by Erica's house. I tried not to cringe at my own behavior. Having to resort to spying on a woman was a severe blow to the confidence of someone of my caliber. Sure, I'd followed her home, but I refused to see it as stalking per se. I had my reasons.

I had put off choosing a target for so long, but my time was running out. Just a few short weeks ago, I'd felt stone dust on the tips of my hair. I was turning. The only way to avoid a permanent transformation would be to adhere to the terms of the curse. Aggravated, I ran a hand through my hair and stopped short of ripping it out.

Damn Aranthena and her curse! Banishing me to the human lands after I denied her marriage proposal, and condemning me to life as a statue, something she thought was a befitting punishment for someone with a "stone heart."

That was rich coming from easily the cruelest woman I knew. Her lack of self-awareness was insane. After cheating on countless lovers in Gorantha, she had the *nerve* to curse me for refusing to entertain her. I simply did not trust her to make a loyal partner, never mind a wife someday, and I told her just as much. I suppose that was my ultimate mistake.

No matter, I'd move forward so long as I had a shred of hope left.

My thoughts immediately drifted back to the gorgeous young woman I had met at the cafe. I recalled her telling me her name was Erica. I'd spent days watching her before ever approaching. When Erica wasn't at work, it seemed she spent most of her time at home — no doubt grieving the loss of her relationship with the man who had recently moved out.

I'd always assumed that brokenhearted women jumped at the chance to replace a love lost with someone else, someone better, or at least take comfort in a distraction from the pain. A *rebound*, they called it. But I supposed I was wrong. Earlier, at the coffee shop, I had anticipated a flirtatious meeting that would end with us swapping numbers. Yet, strangely, Erica didn't seem as taken with me as I'd hoped. Maybe I should have gone for her friend, who was practically eye-fucking me...

No, Erica was a suitable target. Her heart was pure, and it helped that she was fucking gorgeous. Deep almond-shaped eyes, rich sepia brown skin, full lips, and a perfect, curvy, yet slim body. She looked like a goddess. I wouldn't mind fucking her to get out of this curse. I'd blame Erica's aloof demeanor on my poor timing, coupled with the bleakness of mid-December in this land. Apparently, seasonal depression was a real thing for humans. It probably didn't help that she was working long shifts at a coffee shop with the holidays just around the corner, either ...

I moved to get a better view as my target exited her car and nearly tripped over a large stick in the process. I regained my balance quickly and froze, trying to remain quiet. Erica's head snapped in my direction, and I saw her rush into her home, hastily slamming the door behind her.

Erica

I slipped into my favorite chunky cardigan and brewed a hot cup of espresso. I inhaled the aroma and closed my eyes, hoping to push away the feeling of dread that had settled in since last night. I was alone in this empty house, but I was determined to make it my own. The pressure on my foot and an eager meow stirred me out of my thoughts.

"Oh, Luna!" I bent down and stroked her black fur. "At least I'm not totally alone. Jonathon did one good thing by giving you to me for my birthday last year."

I filled up her meal bowls and then scanned the room around me. Finally, I noticed the clutter all around me. Takeout boxes lined the coffee table, dishes piled high in the sink, and garbage spilled from the bin under the sink and littered the floor. Although the thought of using my day off to clean was far from inviting, I knew a fresh home would bring back some clarity of mind, if nothing else. Rolling up my sleeves, I got to work.

An hour and a half later, things were looking much better. I could feel my spirits lifting a little enough that when I found some Christmas decorations in the closet, I decided to set them out. I even lit a few pomegranate-scented candles before looking around and admiring my space.

This place looks so cute and smells fantastic! But soon, the invasive thoughts began and ruined the vibe. "Wish I had someone to appreciate this with me." I kicked myself inwardly.

I lambasted over how much free time being single afforded me. Earlier this year, I'd spent so much time planning our vacation and our wedding, and then fighting with Jonathan, trying to save our relationship as I felt him slip away. But I couldn't save it alone, and our relationship inevitably fell apart. Now, there was nothing to look forward to. No one to plan with and nothing to fight about. Crazy as it sounded, I missed it all, the good and the bad.

Days like today made me want to pick up more shifts at Brewed Luxe and at least earn some extra income. Having free time to sit around and feel sad was exhausting. I unconsciously rubbed my ring finger as I debated how to spend the rest of the day. My eyes shifted to my canvas bag full of old library books that had been sitting by the door for ages. I'd meant to return them but never made the time.

That changes today, I decided.

"Library it is."

Returning old library books was a great excuse to get out of the house. And it was quiet. Something I embraced. Quietness was a direct contrast to my customer service job.

I grabbed my keys and my bag of library books and then set off.

The library had a pleasantly old-fashioned feel, and the atmosphere was tranquil. After returning my books, I decided to stay and browse for a while. There was just something about being amongst the bookshelves that always brought me peace. It was the smell of old books, and the discovery of authors I never would have heard of otherwise. I loved reading, and while I had countless ebooks on my phone I was working through, they simply couldn't replace the feeling of holding a book in my hands. I also liked observing people in the library, seeing moms with their kids and people immersed in their own little worlds, as they typed away on the computers or flipped through the pages of books.

As I wandered down the adult fiction aisle, a distantly familiar voice came up behind me.

"Erica?"

I froze and turned around slowly.

Fuck! It was Johnathan.

Since when did he come to the library? I hadn't known him to set foot in a library for our entire relationship. This was literally the last place I'd expect to run into him.

He was smiling happily, as though nothing was wrong, as though he hadn't broken off our engagement not too long ago. I strained a fake smile of my own and noticed that he was holding a few children's books in one arm. My stomach sank. There weren't a lot of explanations for that.

"Johnathan ... what are you doing here?" I asked, not moving any closer to him.

He looked around guiltily. "I was just..."

"Johnny!" A voice trilled from the kids section. I saw his coworker, Magda, approach him. Magda quickly noticed me.

"Oh ... hey, girl," Magda said, feigning friendliness, as she surveyed me up and down. "Johnathan was just picking out some books to read to my niece."

"Oh, that's nice – " I lied. I didn't care, and I'm sure she could tell.

"Having a good holiday season so far?" she went on. "It's been decent weather-wise, but I heard it's gonna snow later this week. Thank *goodness*, we're leaving for Tulum in a couple of days, right babe?"

My grip on my tote bag tightened.

"Oh, so you're going to Tulum after all, Jonathan?" I asked him bluntly, unable to control my annoyance. "I thought it was too stressful of a trip for you." *Like our wedding.*

"He's had a change of heart," Magda said bitingly. "His choice of company has improved."

"Magda," Jonathan said in a soft reprimand. She rolled her eyes.

I stared at them, feeling the blood in my veins boiling, completely unable to speak. Just then, a buttery, smooth voice called me from behind.

"Erica, darling, there you are."

And as I turned, I saw the man from yesterday at the coffee shop striding up to me. I realized at once that I'd forgotten his name.

He stood beside me and casually draped an arm across my shoulders. Johnathan's eyes nearly bulged out of his head, and Magda was staring from him to me to the stranger, speechless. Looking as confused as I felt, I couldn't help the delight I felt at Johnathan and Magda's unconcealed chagrin.

"What? And who the hell is this, Erica?" Jonathan asked me, and I could hear the controlled anger in his tone.

"The name's Devin. And you can address me directly," Devin said in a voice that took my breath away. *Holy shit.*

"I-I … oh. Well, I see..." Johnathan sputtered, no doubt feeling as stupid as he looked. He glared at me as though he wanted to accuse me of something. What, exactly, was a mystery to me. *He* was the one who cheated on me with the coworker who was "just his office buddy" and "nothing to worry about." Then, he had the nerve to come to my place of peace with his new chick! He deserved to be humiliated.

"Nice to meet you, Devin," my ex said once he had collected himself. "Erica didn't tell me she was with someone, is all," he grumbled under his breath.

"Well, she isn't beholden to you anymore," Devin said with an innocent smile. "But yes, we're on a library date before heading off to dinner, and then, we'll make the most of this cuddle weather," he added suggestively, giving my shoulder a squeeze.

"That's very sweet," Magda cut in. "I'm Magda, by the way," she told Devin, who nodded. "Um, Jonathan, I think we've got enough books for Bethany. Let's go honey."

They awkwardly scrambled away, though their air of haughtiness had fled before them.

I pulled away from Devin's embrace when they were out of sight and sound. With my hands firmly placed on my hips, I faced him fully.

"*You*," I uttered with far more bite in my voice than I'd intended. My typical impulsive nature was taking over. "Are you following me?"

My boldness was not lost on him; his eyebrows jutted up in bewilderment as though the suggestion was absurd. "There is no rule that states you're the only person allowed at the public library."

I felt mild chagrin for even asking, yet I didn't let it stop me from pushing for answers. "It's just... this coincidence is rather strange – like fate, maybe."

He heaved an exhausted sigh. "Well, I'm a firm believer in fate myself, actually. Life is often stranger than fiction."

"How did you know it was me?"

"Hm? I was wandering the aisles after returning some books when I heard a familiar voice. I recognized it as being yours from the cafe. When I saw what was happening ... I knew I had to intervene. And here we are."

"Here we are," I mumbled, stunned at how fortunate his timing had been.

Devin motioned toward the end of the aisle where Johnathan and Magda had departed moments ago with an inquisitive look on his face. "Ex-lover?"

"Just my ex-fiancé and the co-worker he told me not to worry about."

"He seems like an idiot."

I crossed my arms against my chest and stared Devin down, amused that he'd taken such an interest in my affairs. "And what would make you think that?"

He stepped forward and tucked one of my braids behind my ear, sending hot sparks through me - all the way down to my toes. His smoldering eyes met mine as he responded in a low voice. "Because you're easily the most beautiful woman I've ever laid eyes on - and no intelligent man would be stupid enough to let you go."

"If you're trying to flatter me, it's working," I told him light-heartedly.

He shook his head firmly once in disagreement and whispered, "Erica, I am not trying to flatter you. It's just a fact."

I felt my cheeks grow warm at his words, and a coy smile played on my lips. Even if it had been a sweet lie concocted to make me feel better, it felt nice to hear at a time like this.

"You know," started Devin suddenly, his demeanor shifting from serious to light and playful, piquing my curiosity. I looked up to see a broad smile illuminating his face. "Why don't we really go out and have a good time?" his voice was dripping with mischievousness. "Let's show the idiot that he no longer has any power over you. That you're living an enjoyable life without him. I'm sure he'll be devastated if today was anything to go by. Plus, a lovely woman like yourself deserves to be happy. It is almost the holidays, after all."

I couldn't help the smile that tugged at my lips at his words. He did drive a hard bargain, and it didn't hurt that he was so distractingly attractive. But, I stubbornly held on to my earlier sentiments. "Devin, you're very sweet, but I'm not that interested in dating right now. I'm still fresh out of a relationship, and I don't even know you anyway..."

"Erica," he said, and my name rolled off his tongue with ease as though he were familiar with me. "We've met twice now, and I don't believe I'd be reaching if I said there's some chemistry between us," he added with an annoyingly dazzling smile that damn near lit up the room.

I shook my head, enamored by his self-confidence and self-awareness yet irritated by him all the same. He knew exactly the effect he had on people.

"If you'll accept me, I would like the chance to get to know you, take you out. It doesn't have to be a 'date.' It can be completely low-pressure."

I sighed aloud, taking in his gorgeous features once more - his flawless, smooth skin and dark curls. He was clean-cut, sweet, and protective. He didn't seem like a serial killer ... not like they usually did. I thought of Stevie, how easy-going and casual she was when dealing with men, and how her relationships were largely positive. And, once they stopped being enjoyable, how swiftly she would end them without a second thought. She never took her partners seriously enough to grow too attached and get hurt by them. Her level of detachment was actually a little concerning, but she couldn't relate to my heartbreak, so she had to be doing something right.

I took a deep breath and closed my eyes, trying to channel some of her personality at that moment. I exhaled slowly and opened my eyes to find Devin looking at me with a kind sort of patience on his face.

I looked into his gentle eyes. His full lips curved into a little smile, and immediately, something in me stirred at the thought of getting to know him more intimately. I shivered with anticipation.

"All right. What did you have in mind?" I asked him, trying to sound more nonchalant than I felt.

"A nice dinner at my favorite restaurant," came his easy reply. "And naturally, it's on me," Devin added, punctuating his sentence with a playful wink. At that moment, I found myself starting to become drawn to the man before me.

"Naturally," I agreed. "It better be good. I will judge you based on your favorite eatery," I said, half-serious.

He laughed good-naturedly. "Then I won't disappoint. We'll meet at Parallel 37 tonight at seven o'clock," he said. We exchanged phone numbers before he turned away, leaving me alone with thoughts of our upcoming rendezvous flooding my mind.

It only hit me once he was gone that he had invited me to the more expensive restaurant in town. It made me wonder just who this mysterious man was. My excitement for our not-date rose as I chose a few books from the library, checked them out, and headed to my car, stomach fluttering the entire time.

I had to admit I was grateful to Devin. If not for him, I might still be sulking about my run-in with Johnathan and his new girl. But, now I had something positive to look forward to in my own life. If only for a few hours, I felt the potential of a future life I could lead outside the walls of my sorrows.

Tonight, I would sit at a table in a lovely restaurant with a man I barely knew. He was moving fast, no doubt, but I found myself eagerly awaiting the evening ahead.

Chapter Three

Devin

I collapsed across the sofa in the living room of the apartment where I'd been living since the start of my banishment, staring up at the high ceiling.

I had to admit that Erica's resolve impressed me today. She was honest, brutally so. She put her foot down and made it clear where she stood. She was not interested in dating and had no intention of using me as a distraction for her ex.

"It was kind of sexy how she put me in my place," I mused aloud. Still, I'm glad she didn't completely turn me down. It wasn't easy to convince her to go out with me. Erica, I had no problem admitting, was beautiful, stunningly so, and a little feisty as well, which was just hot. Above all, though, she seemed like a genuine and pure-hearted person.

I felt a strange stab of guilt in my gut. *I was absolutely using her, but why did this bother me?*

With every passing day in this realm, I strengthened my resolve to lift the curse. It was all I could afford to care about. I had no time to pity anyone but myself and my family, I decided.

As I stretched across the cushions, my mind wandered back to the confrontation at the library. I stifled a laugh as I remembered what an absolute loser Jonathan seemed to be. Seeing her ex's bewilderment and rage at my presence had been rather satisfying.

I moved across the room towards the large mahogany cabinet. My fingers trembled as I reached for the gold handle and tugged it open. Inside, surrounded by books, was the scrying bowl I used to make and receive calls back home. I took a deep breath and reached in, pulling out the bowl with both hands before setting it on the glass table.

Closing my eyes, I focused on channeling Duran by imagining his face as clear as day in my mind's eye. Slowly, Duran's face came into focus - pale skin, big hazel eyes, and wavy brown hair. His expression changed from calm to shock as soon as he recognized me.

"Duran," I greeted him cautiously. "It's been too long since we last spoke. How are you?"

He shook his head quickly, still trying to process the sight of me after so long apart. "Where've you been?!" he whispered anxiously. "We've been worried about you ever since your exile. I can't sense you -"

" - I'm in the human lands," I cut in.

His voice rose slightly. "Don't tell me you're actually trying to find a human to use and break the curse!"

I fell silent.

"Devin, you're just playing into her game!"

"What other choice do I have, Duran!" I whispered back in a rushed, frustrated tone. "She's taken everything from me. I can't go back home. I can't even publicly speak to my own family and friends. I'm a pariah until I can fix this."

"We could petition for her family to break the curse. We could seek out a powerful magic user here in our lands who can break it. Why are you doing this alone?"

"Because your suggestions could endanger us both!" I countered. "... I've burdened our family enough. You have a lot on your plate. I couldn't possibly ask you to get involved in my mess."

A pause, "Then why did you call me?"

"I just wanted to give you an update. I'm not dead. I'm just getting things sorted out."

He seemed hesitant to ask but found the courage to say, "Will you be home soon?"

"...I will," I told him.

He sighed audibly. "All right, brother. But do keep in touch with me regularly from here on out."

"You too, Duran. Tell Danae I said 'hi.'"

Erica

I could hardly believe that Devin suggested the restaurant known as Parallel 37 for a first date.

When I had spoken to Stevie about it on the phone, she nearly screamed, "That's some real hot girl shit, Erica." When I laughed at her reply, she had doubled down, saying, "I mean it, that restaurant is fancy as hell."

Admittedly, I was excited about tonight. It was a distraction I could use right now, especially after seeing Johnathan and Magda at the library, of all places. Wanting to avoid being underdressed, I did a little social media investigating before putting together my outfit. Finally, I settled on my favorite black sequin midi dress under my grey faux fur coat. I wore my braids in a half-up, half-down do, and topped it off with red lipstick and the gold stud earrings my father had gifted me when I graduated high school years ago.

I arrived at Parallel 37 right on time. As I left my car, I felt my phone vibrate in my clutch. It was a text from Devin that said he was waiting for me outside.

As I approached the building, he stood tall and alluring in a chic, signature Italian flannel suit jacket, his hair perfectly coiffed, beaming as he waved happily at me. I smiled back.

"You look stunning, Erica," he spoke softly.

"Thanks," I said genuinely, "you're not so bad yourself." He smirked and did not attempt to conceal the way his eyes hungrily roamed over my form, before he took the side of my arm and guided me inside the upscale restaurant. Being this close to him, Devin's scent hit me - a mixture of woodlands and citrus.

The hostess smiled kindly as we entered the restaurant. We followed her to our table; the soft yellow light of the candles danced across the walls, until we reached our table in front of a window that featured a magnificent view of the city skyline. Its lights sparkled like stars in the night sky.

As we sat down, I saw that Devin had already ordered a wine for the table. My eyes went wide as I recognized the kind - Penfold Quantum 2018. I'd never seen it for less than one thousand dollars. Is this guy for real?

"Thought I'd start us off with some red wine," Devin, who noticed me gawking at the bottle, piped up. "Hope that's all right."

"I-I, no, it's perfectly fine," I answered, trying to pick my jaw up off the floor and act normal. "It's just ... you spent a pretty penny on this bottle. A whole rack, actually..."

Devin's face relaxed at this, and his pleasant laugh filled my ears. "That's nothing," he said, picking up the bottle and opening it. "Just wanted to get something special for someone I consider special."

He explained as he took my glass, filled it, and handed it to me before serving his own.

He raised his glass, and I followed him. "To new beginnings," he said, and we clinked glasses.

I took a sip of wine. It tasted like nothing I had tried before. There was none of the bitterness of cheaper wines that reminded one they were drinking old grapes. Instead, it had a fruity, smoky taste.

"Good, right?" asked Devin with a wink, already knowing the answer.

I smiled broadly. "It's delicious."

"I thought you'd like it. Let's get some food."

It took us only a short time to choose. We settled on steaks, potatoes, and grilled vegetables.

It occurred to me that Johnathan had never showered me with this kind of expense before. He never went out of his way to impress me or spoil me. When we lived together, everything was split down the middle: bills, dates, right down to our trip to Tulum, Mexico. He used to say he was just "careful with money." I chalked it up to him just being conservative and frugal with his spending. He used to compliment me on how "practical" and "easy-going" I was. But ... it didn't escape me that earlier today, when his new girl spoke of their upcoming trip, it sounded like Johnathan was paying for the whole thing.

I guess it was never about being careful with his spending. Maybe he just never saw me as good enough to treat to nice things. Maybe Stevie was right; a man would only go all out for his dream girl. Devin, on the other hand, not only seemed kind, protective, and eager to know me, but he obviously saw me as valuable enough to deserve nice things. Things I'd never experienced in the four years with my ex. And I convinced myself I didn't care just so I wouldn't feel so sad about it.

I took more sips of wine, the pleasant flavor bursting in my mouth, contrasting something nauseating that twisted in my stomach.

"You all right?" asked Devin, "you're a little quiet."

"Actually," I started. What do you really want from me, Devin? Who falls this hard and fast? I'm a stranger to you, yet you're treating me like a spoiled princess. Or maybe I'm just so used to being treated subpar that my expectation bar is in hell. "Devin," I began again, "Let me ask you something."

"Generally, what people do on first dates."

"Wait, I thought this wasn't a date."

Devin's lips curled up in a sexy smirk as he responded, "My mistake. I meant 'first not-date.'"

"Right..." I felt a heat sparking from his gaze as I ventured, "So, what made you ask me out?"

For the first time since I met him, Devin appeared a little shy. A boyish smile tugged at his lips as his gaze dropped to his plate, and he cut into his steak. When his answer came, it was simple yet genuine, "Because you're gorgeous, kind, and have a captivating energy that lights up any room you walk into." He looked up at me at this. "You don't realize your own power, Erica."

I tried not to let his words affect me too much. I didn't need his flattery. Though, I couldn't deny the satisfaction I felt hearing my name fall from his lips like a prayer.

I tasted the savory mashed potatoes, and as I swallowed, Devin's hand clutched mine. His touch sent a jolt of electricity through me. I could feel my heart racing and desire coursing through my body. Those eyes, intense and filled with want, captivated me.

He was hot--so very hot. Kind, too--and he had the obvious means to spoil me rotten if I wanted him to. There was no hesitation in his gaze or his grip on my hand.

"Take a chance on me," he said with an intensity that made my heart skip another beat. I slowly entwined our fingers, allowing myself to bask in the comfort of this moment.

Oh, what the hell. Might as well have some fun with this, I decided.

"One chance," I responded in agreement, suddenly feeling endangered by the promise of pleasure that lurked beneath the surface of his words. "Just don't fuck me over," I warned half-seriously.

"There's only one way I'd do that, and you'd like it," he replied in a low voice, which sent a shiver down my spine. The air around us felt heavy with sexual tension but somehow still inviting and comforting.

We shared Baked Alaska for dessert and talked about our family lives, though I didn't press when Devin told me he was from quite far away.

The desire between us was palpable now. I knew better than to trust him too soon, but his presence wrapped around me like a warm blanket on a cold night and imbued my soul with hope again. This was, after all, way better than moping around my empty apartment. Maybe this was the start of something new.

"What are your plans for Christmas?" I asked between bites of rich ice cream and sponge cake.

He paused, pondering, with his spoon still halfway in his mouth. Carefully, he placed it on the porcelain plate before him and lifted a shoulder in a shrug. "I don't have many. We never celebrated it back home."

"Are you up for celebrating it this year? Now that you're here?" I asked, hopeful.

"Maybe," he said, smiling slowly. "What do you like about this holiday?"

Fond memories of my youth flooded my brain. "One of my favorite traditions is decorating the Christmas tree. I have ornaments I've been collecting since I was a kid. When we were young, my dad used to blast Christmas music while we all decorated the tree together and drank sorrel with roasted chestnuts and gingerbread cookies."

"That's a beautiful memory," said Devin, admiring my liveliness and joy. He thought for a moment before adding, "I've never heard of sorrel before."

"Oh! It's this delicious hibiscus and rum-based drink they make during the holidays in Jamaica - that's where my mom is from. It's really good. It's sweet, and the ginger adds a nice kick. It's really addictive, and its red coloring makes it really festive. My sister and I would help our mom make it every year. We ... we felt like a real family in those moments." Lost in memories, I nearly missed Devin regarding me with a wistful gaze.

"Family is the most important thing in the world, isn't it?" he said reverently.

I thought about my sister, my parents, my cousins, the rest of my extended family, and those precious moments during Christmas growing up. "It is."

Soon, we had finished dessert, and Devin was paying our tab. He must have tipped our waitress handsomely because when he handed her back the debit machine, her eyes widened in surprise, and she said, "Thank you. Bless you." It was definitely a green flag.

We rose from the table, Devin towering over me in a way that made me feel safe. His eyes seemed to shine in the low lighting of the restaurant.

"I'll walk you to your car," he offered quietly before leading the way outside. I couldn't help but be surprised by his gallantry; no seductive invitations for drinks at bars or his place? Impressive.

When we arrived at my car, I faced him with a bit of reluctance. I knew this was the part where we should say our goodbyes. But instead, I leaned into him. Instantly, warmth engulfed my body as his strong arms embraced me, his hands resting gently against my back. At that moment, I felt the urge to cry come over me.

That's when I kissed him - suddenly, impulsively - and without warning. He seemed taken aback for a second before responding with comforting fervency, one hand cupping my face while the other moved to the back of my neck in a firm yet gentle grasp.

As if a jolt of electricity had been released through my bloodstream, I felt every muscle quiver in excitement as I pressed down on his abdomen - all hard muscles and solid strength - before locking my arms tightly around his waist. My heart drummed wildly as we kissed, heat radiating between us.

We broke free for a moment and locked eyes, our souls intertwined in search of something magical. I couldn't believe I was so daring as to make out with my date right in front of my car. And what's more, I couldn't believe I was actually considering sleeping with him tonight. Never had I gone home with someone on the first date; it always seemed like an act of impatience, spontaneity, and recklessness. But ... hadn't I been straying from my comfort zone a lot lately? And, things had worked out better than

I expected. So why not now? How many chances like this would come along in life?

Devin's gaze held me captive, his eyes full of alluring curiosity and something supernatural. He looked upon me like I was a divine being as his strong hands gripped my waist and pulled me closer to him. A burning sensation spread through my body as if he were transferring his own desire onto me, making me feel wanted and alive.

He pulled me back in to kiss tenderly, and I felt his rigid heat against my lower abdomen. I reached down and caressed his dick with my hand through his pants. The sound that escaped him would echo in my memories forever.

"Erica," he said, his voice ragged against my neck, "we don't have to—tonight—if it's too soon..." The fact that his self-control was still intact, even as I massaged his throbbing arousal, was all the confirmation I needed.

"I want to, Devin."

"Do you now?" I heard a tinge of joy in his voice, and I nodded.

"You want what, Erica? Specify."

I smiled despite myself; I knew others perceived me as reserved. But not here, not now.

"I want you to fuck me properly."

Devin groaned and scooped me up into his arms, and pressed my body against the car as he kissed me passionately. His hands explored my neck and cupped my breast; I moaned uncontrollably into his mouth.

"If you keep talking that way, I'm gonna do you right here in this parking lot, Erica darling." Devin's panting breaths continued to make me feverish with anticipation.

I laughed lightl. "I prefer a bed when there's one available."

He matched my energy, grinning devilishly at the suggestion. He leaned in so I felt his warm breath against my ear, and whispered, "That can be arranged."

He gently carried me to his car.

Chapter Four

Erica

Before long, we arrived at Devin's high-rise apartment soon enough. The elevator opened up to a lavish two-bedroom luxury home, with wall to ceiling windows and polished hardwood flooring.

He led me to his bedroom, a gorgeous yet minimalistic style room with a king-sized bed and chic night tables. A window was situated on the wall adjacent to the bed, where two Monstera plants sat on the floor on either side of it. Across the room was his closet, and an antique dresser and mirror. Finally, there was another door that I could only assume led to his bathroom.

We fell onto the white, Egyptian cotton sheets of his bed, and he pressed his hard body against mine, pushing me into the firm mattress beneath us. His kisses were like fire as we explored each other's mouths, and I wrapped my legs around him in desperation.

The heat between us was palpable as Devin's lips continued down my decollete. With each kiss and nibble, I felt more and more aroused until I was aching for him with an intensity I'd never felt before.

"Devin," I muttered, breathless. "Want you so bad."

Devin stepped back from me slightly, looking into my eyes. The passion in his gaze burned bright, and I felt my heart beat faster in anticipation of what might come next.

"So impatient," Devin chided, laughing softly. His voice was suddenly more serious. "Erica, you have no idea what you do to me. I can barely control myself as it is, but if we continue ... I don't think I can hold myself back at all..."

I smiled at this, pleased to know that I affected him just as much as he did me. I took down the rest of my braids from my half-up ponytail, so they cascaded over my shoulders and framed my face. I tilted my head seductively, knowing he was watching my every move, "You promise?"

"Be careful, darling," he chuckled. "There's no going back if you really want this. Do you want me to fuck you? You can change your mind right now, but not after."

My heart was beating so quickly that I swore I could hear it pounding in my ears. I knew there was something a little wild about Devin, something he seemed to be suppressing under his kind, laid-back, and polite demeanor. At that moment, it felt like his mask had slipped, and he was warning me that he had no intention of putting it back on if we continued. Part of me felt like I should be a little wary, a little anxious. I had never seen him so dominant.

When I pulled myself out of my thoughts, I found Devin watching me, waiting for my answer. I nodded in reply, but he grabbed my chin in his hand with a slight growl and leaned over me so our faces were inches apart.

"Say it."

"I want you. All of you. Don't hold bac – "

That seemed to be all he needed to hear as he crashed our lips together before I could finish.

I snaked my hand up his neck and through Devin's hair, kissing him back just as deeply. He ran his hands over my breasts, caressing them teasingly, before roaming over the soft curves of my waist and hips. I let out a soft moan, overcome with desire for him. I slid out of my dress and reached for his shirt, and he took the hint right away, tearing open his shirt in a way that I could only describe as feral, revealing an impressive build, complete with big, toned arms and chiseled abs.

He winked at me playfully, and I watched him in awe, and need as he unbuckled his belt and hastily rid himself of his pants, so that only his black silk boxers remained.

I reached for them, but he held my hands firmly, looking at me with a hungry stare.

"I wanna taste you," he said simply. And with that, he moved on top of me, kissing down my stomach and continuing lower and lower until I felt the warmth of his breath against the fabric of my panties. He slid them down ever-so-slowly until they had been entirely removed from my body. My legs trembled as anticipation built up inside me, but then suddenly, I felt the heat of his tongue against my clit. Pleasure instantly radiated from my body.

His tongue explored every inch of my folds until I felt it plunged deep into my pussy, while his hands roamed freely over my skin, causing little sparks of electricity wherever they touched. His touch was gentle yet demanding; I could feel myself responding to him instinctively, wanting more and more as his mouth moved over me like a wildfire spreading across my skin.

My breath came in short gasps as Devin's tongue expertly explored delicious places within me—places I hadn't even realized existed before—causing sensations that had been previously unknown to course through my body like a wild lightning storm.

The pleasure was almost too much to bear, and I could feel myself nearing the edge as Devin's mouth continued its exploration. My hands found purchase in his hair, and I grabbed it fistfuls, but he stopped just before I could reach my climax.

I let out a frustrated moan, and to my surprise, he laughed in response. His fingertips slowly grazed my sensitive clit, sending shivers through my body but not enough to get me off.

Devin's eyes met mine, a smirk playing on his lips as he noticed his effect on me. He shifted his body slightly until his hardness pressed against my softness, and I could feel myself growing even more aroused.

His hands traveled from my hips to my waist, and then cupped my face in his hands.

His gaze became even more intense as he whispered, "Beg me, princess. Tell me how much you need me to make you explode ..."

I swallowed thickly. I could feel myself trembling in anticipation. I knew what he was asking for, and without a word, I looked into his eyes and softly said, "Please make me come, Dev ... I need it so badly ..."

He smiled knowingly before bending down to kiss me once more. His tongue began tracing circles around mine as his fingers started to skillfully massage my clit in slow circles. My breathing hitched, and I could feel the pleasure building up inside of me until it was almost unbearable.

Desperately, I begged him again, this time louder than before, "Please make me come..."

He moved back and lowered his boxers. I was met with what I can only describe as the biggest cock I'd ever seen in my life. He had to be ten inches, definitely over eight. It was surreal. I reached out, and this time he let me touch him. His length was heavy, rock solid, standing at attention and dripping pre-cum. I encircled his length with my fingers, noting how thick he was as well. I stroked him only a few times before he grunted and pushed me down on the bed, trapping my body beneath him.

"Like what you see, hm?"

"You're so big."

He smirked, amused by my comment. "You have no idea. Scared?"

I shook my head. "But be gentle," I told him. I was more than a little unsure if his monster cock would fit inside me without issue. Where was all that length supposed to go anyway? My stomach? "I've never been with someone your size."

"You flatter me," Devin responded, but deep down, we both knew it was true. "Don't worry. I'm gonna make you feel so good," he promised.

He stroked his cock over my pussy lips, sending waves of pleasure through us both before gently pushing at my entrance. Though he was gentle, I could feel myself being completely stretched wide open. I gritted my teeth.

"Breathe," he told me softly as he continued to fill me up, inch by inch.

When he penetrated fully within me, he uttered a low, satisfied groan that sent tremors up my spine. I closed my eyes and embraced the unfamiliar sensation of being filled so wholly. It was almost too much. I had never felt so filled in my life. I tried to remember his words and took deep, long breaths, trying to adjust to his length and thickness.

He gave me no more time to adjust as he started to move in and out of me with smooth and deliberate thrusts. His hips swiveled with practiced ease as he worked his dick deep inside me. I gripped his shoulders desperately to gain purchase. I couldn't help but moan loudly as the sensations kept intensifying inside me. He was hitting all the right spots. Every thrust triggered an intensified wave of rapture within my core that caused me to cry out in delirious delight.

He quickened his pace, pushing deeper and harder into me with each thrust. My fingernails dug into his back this time, not wanting him to stop but unable to take much more at this point. The pleasure increased until it became almost unbearable, and I felt like I was going crazy from all the sensations.

Then suddenly, everything stopped – Devin seemed lost in the moment – before he took a deep breath and gave one last powerful thrust, sending us both over the edge together. His lusty grunt pierced my soul before he leaned over and kissed me, swallowing my cries as his thick essence filled me, flooding me with rapturous pleasure.

He continued to fuck me through my climax until another one hit and another. I lost count as wave after wave flowed through me until I was left shaking and spent. Only then did he pull out of me and roll over onto the bed beside me. He pulled me close to him, so my head lay on his muscular chest as we both fell into a blissful post-coital silence.

We lay there, just holding each other tight - savoring every second spent in each other's arms.

"Are you all right?" he spoke after a time, gently stroking my hair.

"Yes," I spoke, my voice smaller than I intended.

He adjusted himself to get a better look at my face. "You're amazing, Erica, you know that?"

For some reason, shyness overcame me, and I buried my face in Devin's chest, taking in the pleasant smell of sandalwood and bergamot radiating off his skin.

"No, you are," I said simply, half-asleep. I felt him chuckle against me.

"Down for the count, huh?"

"Just for now," I told him.

"Don't force yourself," he said teasingly. "I'm a lot to handle sometimes."

I scoffed playfully. "Dev," I spoke up.

"Hm?"

"You should come over to my place next. We can hang out, bake, and decorate my Christmas tree. You'll like it."

His laughter reverberated against me. "You're definitely selling it. Just tell me when, and I'll be there," he said, kissing my forehead.

❧

Devin

Beautiful. Stunning. Perfect. Those were the words that entered my mind as I watched Erica. Absentmindedly, I traced circles over her shoulder with my thumb, admiring her smooth, beautiful brown skin as she lay against my chest. She wasn't sleeping, but I could tell she was tired.

I hadn't been too rough, I told myself. It had taken a lot of restraint not to overwhelm her with my stamina or strength so soon. Back home, I had scared off partners in the past with my enthusiasm at times. I was getting better about that. I wanted her again. Right now. But I would try to restrain myself.

Don't scare her away.

Her gaze shifted up to me, and her rosy, full lips parted before she said, "Do you mind if I get cleaned up?"

"That's no problem," I said earnestly. "Would you like a bubble bath with candles and wine, princess?"

She laughed, the sound pleasant in my ears. "Oh, stop. Seriously, though, where's the bathroom?"

"Follow me," I told her. We rose from the bed together, and she followed me to the master bathroom. I gathered some shower accessories for her: a fresh towel, a washcloth, a shower cap, and soap.

"Whoa," Erica said from behind me. I turned to find her gazing around the spacious room, taking in the maple-brown marble slab walls and flooring, and the colorful succulent plants along the countertop. "This place is gorgeous." She walked over to the free-standing tub next to the large window that provided a spectacular view of the city.

I walked up behind her and kissed her cheek. "Want me to draw you a bath?" I teased.

She turned to me smiling but shook her head. "Just a regular shower is fine. If I took a bath in there, I'd probably never leave this house."

"What's wrong with that?" I asked, throwing her a flirty look.

"I'm sure you'd enjoy it," she said, "but I have work in the morning."

"If you were mine, I'd retire you. You could spend your days soaking in tubs or soaking up the sun on beaches."

She rolled her eyes, but I didn't miss the hint of a smile she tried to conceal.

I'm convinced she thinks I'm joking most of the time, even when I'm being serious. I blame my flirty nature. Since I can't really turn it off, I guess it can't be helped.

Continuing to ignore my confession, she extended her hand expectantly. Taking the hint, I gave her everything in my arms except the clean towel, which I hung on the rack next to the shower.

"Thanks," she said, slipping the cap over her braids before stepping into the shower and closing the glass door.

I turned and left.

Erica

Retire me, huh? Guys will say all types of crazy shit after you let them hit, right until their post-nut clarity, of course.

Besides, while I'd love the idea of never needing to work again, I'd probably still pick up shifts now and then. After all, I liked my work, my co-workers – most of the time – and the general cafe atmosphere.

Hot water showered my body, cleansing the day's sweat and dirt off me. I washed myself from head to toe before relaxing under the stream.

I tried not to think about how fit Devin's body was, but promptly failed. Stevie was right. Devin was so freaking hot, and for what?! His physique was drool-worthy, and he had the perfect proportions, too: strong arms, abs made for licking all over, and those triceps, whew!

"He definitely doesn't skip leg day."

"I'd love to confirm that, but it's mostly good genes."

His voice nearly made me jump out of my skin. I spun around to see Devin standing in the shower doorway with his own washcloth. "Mind if I join you?" he asked.

"It's your house," I replied, making room for him, which wasn't too hard to do in the ample space. I watched, captivated, as he soaped up his washcloth before running the suds-filled over his arms, chest, abs, and ...

I forced myself to turn away and give him privacy, even though he clearly didn't care since he had chosen to shower with me. I thought to steal a peek at him, and embarrassingly enough, I let my intrusive thoughts win. I looked at him just in time to see him leaning into the warmth of the shower stream, as the water cascaded down the column of his neck and over his back.

"You're staring, princess," he teased, turning to me, his hand lifting to caress my hip, sending a jolt of desire up my spine. His head lowered until it was next to my ear, "like what you see?" he whispered, "because I know I do."

He pushed me against the tiled wall behind me. The wet strands of Devin's hair tickled my cheeks as our bodies pressed together firmly. My body tingled at his touch alone.

"You are so beautiful, you know that?" he spoke against my skin.

"Those words coming from Adonis himself, I'm touched," I responded softly and kissed his lips before he tore away from me. I gasped as he dipped his head to leave a trail of hot kisses all over my neck.

Suddenly, he grasped the showerhead and directed its warm spray onto my breasts. His touch electrified my skin, and I let out a loud moan as his hands moved down to my stomach and finally settled between my legs. He brought the stream of water directly over my clit, sending waves of pleasure through me.

"Devin!" I cried as the pleasure built up in my core, "Devin, please!"

In one fluid motion, Devin put the showerhead back on its stand, then let out a low growl. I was pressed harder into the wall with one of Devin's hands grasping my right thigh to lift it over his hip. I wrapped my arms around his neck and the wet strands of his hair tickled my cheeks, as we held each other in a fervid embrace. I could sense his sudden urgency from the moment Devin rolled his hips – straining cock rubbing against my inner thigh.

"I like it when you beg me," he said with a wicked half-smile, grey eyes flashing excitedly. He took his rock-hard cock in one hand and rubbed it up and down my pussy so that I felt the pressure directly over my clit. I moaned and bucked against him, frustrated, to his amusement.

He chuckled at my impatience and guided his free hand upward to caress my breasts as he entered me roughly. I gasped, then moaned from the sudden fullness.

"You're so tight," he said against the back of my neck, and I felt his teeth sharply graze my skin before he slammed into me. I screamed, and my eyes rolled back as he increased the pace. His breathing grew ragged, as did mine.

He pulled out suddenly, and I whimpered at the loss of him.

"Turn around," he instructed. And I did so, sticking out my ass eagerly. He gave me a playful slap. "I love this view," he said before I felt him grip my cheeks harshly in both hands, spreading me. Then, he drove his thick, hard dick back into me once more. This time he shifted his position by bending his knees a little, and angling his hips upward so he could drive his dick deeper into me.

I screamed again as the tip of his dick hit a bundle of nerves that made me lose control. He grabbed one of my hands off the wall by the wrist, pulling it behind my back as he fucked me into oblivion.

"Don't move," he said huskily.

Like I could, even if I wanted to, I was at his mercy. All I could do was moan around his huge dick and take it. Just when I thought I couldn't be any more overwhelmed and overstimulated, I felt a harsh, open-handed slap on my ass. The sound resounded off the walls. I jumped but could do nothing more before I felt another hit.

"You tighten up even more every time I slap your ass," he mocked, "and you're getting so wet. Have I found out a little secret about you?"

The sensations of pleasure mixed with pain had me mesmerized, almost delirious, as he kept pounding into me, each thrust accompanied by a slap on my backside. I was unable to respond.

We moved together with an almost painful intensity. Just when I thought my body could take no more, I stiffened suddenly, crying out as an orgasm burst through me like an erupting volcano. Again, Devin fucked me through it before he pulled out, and I felt hot liquid hit my feverish skin as he came on my back.

I nearly collapsed before he caught me in his arms, spun me around, and kissed me deeply, his hand circling my neck.

"You good?" he asked me gently, a far contrast to the harshness with which he had slapped me just moments before.

"Y-yes," I nodded, breathless. "Just a little sore."

He had the decency to look somewhat remorseful and reached out, rubbing my stinging backside apologetically. "Should I make you a sandwich? Or maybe give you a massage?" he said smiling, quirking an eyebrow suggestively.

I slapped his shoulder lightly. "Just some water."

"Got it."

"But ... you're gonna have to help me clean up again because I can hardly move right now."

He grinned, and if I wasn't so tired, I could have sworn I saw two fangs peeping from beneath his top lip. "Deal," he said blithely.

Devin carried me bridal-style into his bedroom when we finished in the bathroom. After handing me a cold bottle of water, he let me borrow a white T-shirt and a pair of gray slacks to wear to sleep. I pulled them on, savoring the fact that his clothes smelled like him, pleasant, sensual and refreshing. Silently, Devin watched me get dressed from the bed. After I had finished dressing, I held out my arms and twirled around in my makeshift pajamas, feeling like a kid wearing their dad's clothes.

"These are pretty comfy," I said appreciatively.

"You've never looked hotter," said Devin. I snorted at his comment and climbed into the bed to join him. He pulled me close, and we drifted off to sleep in each other's arms.

Chapter Five

Erica

I stirred lazily in Devin's bed, savoring the sweet memories of the night before. I don't think I'd ever experienced that much pleasure. It had been, quite honestly, the best sex I'd ever had. Devin was amazing in so many ways.

Could it be that I was actually be interested in dating Devin? I was shocked that the thought even crossed my mind. I had never been one to get over romantic relationships quickly. I'd only ever had two serious romances in my entire life, and the last one was supposed to result in a marriage to the man I thought was my forever person – Johnathan. Although, he had long moved on and seemed happy, whereas I was still in the mourning phase of our split. Yet, it felt like I was moving out of it faster than I could have imagined. Maybe Stevie was right and the best way to get over someone was to get under someone else. It was working so far anyway.

At that thought, I rolled over, expecting to find Devin beside me. Instead, his side of the bed was empty. I sat up, immediately feeling on guard for some reason. The room was utterly quiet and was shrouded in darkness.

That's weird. What time is it?

Instinctively, I felt around for my cell phone before groaning with despair as I remembered this wasn't my house. I had left my phone in my purse on top of Devin's kitchen counter.

Damn. Now I had no idea what time it was. I could only guess it was a couple hours after midnight. Across the room was an alarm clock, but it faced away from the bed which made it impossible to read from where I sat.

Ugh. Whatever.

Drowsy, I thought about snuggling back into the soft sheets and going back to sleep, when a muffled voice from another room caught my attention. I knew better than to eavesdrop, but I couldn't help myself; my curiosity was piqued. As I listened, it was clear Devin was on a phone call with someone. His enigmatic nature made the temptation to snoop all too great. I crept to the door, and with my ear pressed against the gap, I listened. Devin spoke with an urgency and concern that was obvious, even from a distance.

"-- I know. I know it's been a long time," he agreed. "I've really missed you too. Don't worry, I'll be home soon."

Who did he miss? Another woman? I tried to quell my paranoia. He had mentioned returning home. He must have been having a conversation about his country. There was always that slight, elusive accent in Devin's voice. And, although I had asked him earlier about his homeland, it seemed, for some reason, like he was reluctant to share his origins with me. A twinge of guilt for listening in on him surfaced, but my curiosity - and anxiety - were far too intense to walk away now. Yet nothing, absolutely nothing, could have prepared me for what I heard next.

"How do I know it'll be easy? Because she's recently gone through a breakup. She's vulnerable and could use a knight in shining armor to make her feel loved again. It isn't difficult. ... We had a nice dinner and I just fucked her tonight. I'm already starting to win her over. Soon, she'll fall for me. I can sense it. Human women are not harder to get than any other. Hell, they may be easier. All I need to do is ensure she's completely in love with me. Then, we're home free. Huh? ... Yeah, we can celebrate when I'm back."

I froze.

What. The. Fuck?!

For a moment, I found myself paralyzed. It was too much to process. What had he just said? *Human women?! Make me feel loved again? Starting to win me over? The fuck?!*

My breath caught in my throat. I inched back to the bed. I had heard enough. There was no way I could face Devin after hearing him spewing that bullshit about me. I needed to escape.

Fear had gripped me, a stark, irrational fear. Devin hadn't said anything overtly threatening, but the tone of that conversation... it had every cell in my body screaming at me to flee. That person I had met at the cafe, in the library, at the restaurant, in his home, was not who he was pretending to be. The Devin I knew was a character he was cosplaying. His face a human mask. I realized then that I didn't quite know *who* this person and I didn't want to stick around to find out.

"Just get out of this apartment," I whispered to myself like a mantra, hearing Devin's voice start to fade from the other room. "Just get out of here and go home." But how? It's not like I could just confront him about it right here. I'd heard too many crime stories to think that confronting a strange man about his lies, alone, in his home, was a good idea.

I panicked when I heard Devin moving around in the living room. My mind raced as his foot falls approached the bedroom door. I dove under the covers, throwing them over half my face and feigned sleep. Thankfully, I didn't need to put on much of a show.

Devin entered the bedroom but upon his arrival, he kept the lights off and didn't approach the bed. Instead, he bee-lined for the bathroom and closed the door behind him. Relief washed over me as I heard the sound of tap water running, the sound filling the quiet apartment. It gave me a moment to figure out my next move. My eyes fixed on the door.

This was it. My opportunity. I threw the blanket aside, knowing I had to get out now while I had a chance. I grabbed my dress off the floor, opened the bedroom door carefully, and then bolted into his kitchen to grab my purse. Stuffing my dress inside, I made my way to the front door and hurriedly, slipped into my shoes. I slipped out of his apartment, shutting the door as quietly behind myself as possible.

Walking briskly to the elevator, I pressed the button to descend to the ground floor, and once I was out on the street, I called a cab to take me back to the restaurant parking lot.

"So much for taking chances on strangers," I grumbled bitterly as my cab pulled up. The cab pulled up within minutes and I was so very grateful for its good timing.

"Where to?" asked the cab driver, an older man, portly man with a kind smile. I told him Brewed Luxe, and we arrived shortly after that. From there, I got in my car and drove home.

As I walked through the door, my phone began to go off. It was Devin. I realized I had missed at least five calls from him. And he was calling again now as I stared at my phone screen, but I didn't answer. That's when I was bombarded with a barrage of texts.

Erica??

Where are you? What happened?

Why aren't you answering your phone?

I sent him a quick text back.

I'm fine, just left.

Then I set my phone on the counter, put it on silent, and moved to the couch.

What in the world's going on? I needed time to digest the conversation I had overheard at his place. Now that I was safely back home, the fear began to fade, allowing the memory of Devin's words to replay in my head. The way he bragged about fucking me, about how simple it would be to make me fall for him. I felt a lump form in my throat, thinking about how sweet he had been to my face, contrasted by how crazy he had spoken of me behind my back. *What a complete asshole.*

I didn't even know where to start with his mention of "human women," was that some new derogatory term for women these days, much like the term "modern women" had become thanks to male podcast culture? Honestly, I didn't even care.

My brain was still trying to reconcile the version of Devin I thought I knew from our date — the charming, humorous, intelligent, kind, irresistibly handsome man — with the one I had just overheard. I was desperate for answers, but my trust in Devin was broken.

Maybe I'll contact him again in the morning, I thought as I headed toward bedroom, collapsing onto my bed. But for now, I just needed to rest.

Devin

I had fucked up. That much was clear when I returned from the bathroom and couldn't find Erica anywhere. She must have made a mad dash while I was in the bathroom. A swift exit from Erica had to mean something in our delicate, burgeoning relationship had shifted. She must have overheard some of my conversation. I didn't remember exactly what I might have said that triggered her, but I knew my words had not been kind toward Erica.

I might as well be wearing a stupid sign because that was how I felt.

Erica had stopped answering my calls, and I doubted showing up at her home, when I wasn't supposed to know where she lived, would go over well.

I needed to rectify this quickly. I headed into Erica's workplace, hoping it wasn't one of her days off. Upon my arrival, I spotted Jennifer and Stevie working the registers. I walked up to Stevie. She smirked and diverted her gaze, pointedly avoiding eye contact with me when I joined her line. Patiently, I waited until it was my turn.

"What do you want?" she asked tersely, not even attempting to play dumb or feign politeness.

Of course, Erica would tell her friend. Why wouldn't she?

"Stevie," I started. "I know you must've heard some unsavory things about me, but you've got to help me get in touch with Erica. I think she may have the wrong idea--"

"-- I disagree. I think she's got the idea perfectly *right*. And you think I've *got* to help you?" she repeated, incredulously. "Weren't you basically gloating about using her because you saw her as an emotionally damaged, easy target? You, sir, are sick. *Unhinged.* You can get fucked."

Heads turned in our direction as a few patrons overheard us. Jennifer, who was making drinks, inched closer to eavesdrop on our conversation.

"Hey!" I snapped, partly due to her shocking words and partly due to the volume of her voice. I lowered my own voice. "I swear to the gods, there is so much more to this than what Erica heard. If I could speak with her, I could make things right." Stevie sighed and pointedly looked behind me at other customers in line as if signaling she was over our discussion. I took the hint. "Tell her I dropped by?" I said, feeling a little defeated. "She deserves closure, at least."

Stevie looked me up and down before leaning forward so that only I could hear her. "I guess I could pass on that message ... for a tip." I blinked, puzzled, and she raised an eyebrow at me.

Ah. A bribe. I didn't even allow myself to get upset. If this was what it took to talk to Erica again, so be it. I reached into my pocket and brandished a one hundred dollar bill, dropping it straight into her outstretched palm. Stevie snatched it with lightning speed, crumpled it, and stuffed it in the pocket of her apron.

"I *knew* you were rich. Take a seat. Erica's shift starts a little later. I'll make sure to warn her you're here."

"Warn her?" I repeated. *Weird choice of words.*

"Yeah," said the young woman, "You know, in case Erica wants to bail. You're not entitled to her time. Now go on." She shooed me out of line.

Guess I wouldn't be given the privilege of ordering coffee today. I sat at a corner table and felt my stomach twist in a hint of panic as I waited for Erica to arrive. I had fucked everything up. After overhearing my conversation, I was horrified at what she must think of me. It dawned on me then that it wasn't even the curse I was most concerned about, but rather, I honestly cared what Erica thought of me as a person. The thought of hurting her riddled me with guilt.

She really likes me. ...Or, rather, she did. Now, I wasn't so that confident.

The thought of falling out of favor with her bothered me. Yet, I could not allow myself to fall in love with Erica. It was too troublesome. If I developed such feelings, how could I leave the human lands and return home to my family? I couldn't abandon them. Erica and I had bonded over many things, including the importance of family connection. The memory of her recalling the blissful moments she spent with her loved ones, enjoying Christmast traditions over the years, filled me with regret. How could I have caused her such pain? Was I truly any better than her vile, stupid and selfish ex?

I cursed softly as I gazed out the window at the falling snow. It was approaching my second year here, and much like the first, the holiday season in the human lands never ceased to feel cold and isolating.

Like your stone heart, came Aranthena's voice in my head. Maybe she'd been right about me all along. Perhaps I was just a cold-hearted statue, undeserving of love.

Erica

I sat on my couch watching a rerun of one of my comfort shows while Luna slumbered blissfully in my lap. I felt a calm wave wash over me as I absentmindedly ran my fingers through her soft fur. A gentle vibration next to us brought me from my reverie. I grabbed my phone to see a message from Stevie.

Girl, your rich, hot stranger is in the shop today waiting for you. You've been warned. Oh! I scammed him out of a hundred bucks, so drinks on me soon.

I stared at the phone screen, dreading what to do about my shift this evening. I was too emotionally mature to ghost someone I'd slept with, and something told me that Devin would not be ignored easily anyway. I decided then that it was time to officially end things. I felt foolish for getting myself into this mess, but I supposed it couldn't be helped. Taking a deep breath, I reluctantly got dressed and left the house.

When I pulled into the cafe, I could see Devin sitting at a corner table near the windows. He looked haggard like he had barely slept. He alternated between sitting down and tapping his foot, and standing up and pacing.

He's probably annoying everyone in the cafe. I sighed, and entered my workplace.

Devin spotted me right away, and before he could make a scene, I walked over and sat across from him. It was now or never.

"Devin, this morning I heard – "

"– Erica," he cut me off. "I know what you heard, and it wasn't like that. *Really.*"

I leaned back in my seat, arms folded across my chest. "So what exactly was it like? How was I supposed to take being disrespected like that?"

He took a breath and ran a hand through his hair, before leaning in closely to avoid being overheard. He spoke quietly, "To make a really long story short, I'm not exactly from here – here being your Earth, I mean. Anyway, back where I'm from, there's a woman with a lot of power and influence. I angered her a couple of years ago and, for that, she compromised the livelihoods of my siblings by confiscating our family home and assets should I fail to complete a certain task. Time's running out. As the eldest, it weighs on me that I can't do more for my brother and sister right now. I said those awful things unthinkingly. I was only trying to reassure my brother that I would be home soon. It doesn't represent how I truly feel about you. ... Still, I never should have spoken about you that way – "

" – What certain task are you talking about?" I interrupted him in a voice louder than I intended. "And why the hell should I believe you would speak dishonestly to your own brother but save the truth for me, the vulnerable girl you met just days ago? That doesn't make any sense, and you know it."

"I know, you're right, Erica..." he spoke quietly. "But it's the truth. I just wanted to keep my siblings hopeful while I tried to work things out. As for the task, well, on top of wanting to confiscate my family's assets, the woman placed a life-altering curse on me. So, now I must break it if I hope for anything close to a normal life again."

"Okay," I spoke softly but firmly, and held up my hand to silence him. Thankfully he stopped talking. "Okay." This had gone far enough.

There was a thick silence between us as I searched his eyes for a shred of sanity or reason. Devin seemed so serious about his ridiculous story it was almost impressive. He was either terribly insane, or he thought I was terribly stupid. Possibly both. I felt a wave of irritation and anger rush through my blood at the thought that he had chosen such a serious moment as this to play games with me. Was this truly his plan — to convince me of a fantastical story so I'd excuse his selfish and despicable behavior? No man had ever dared to insult me like this. Hell, not even Johnathan thought me this dense.

"Nice try, but you're not gonna gaslight me with stories of evil curses. This isn't some children's fairytale where you can blame your actions on magical misfortunes. *Grow the hell up*!" I stood up as he remained seated, so he was looking up at me as my eyes pierced his. "It's insulting that you ever thought I'd fall for this. Wasting my time. Don't talk to me again."

"Erica, wait," he said, rising from his seat as well and crowding me as if to block me from leaving. "I'm not gaslighting you. I swear it. Every word I said was true. Every word."

"Back off!" I said, my voice more assertive than I felt. He hesitated, then took a step back. I brushed past him silently, making my way behind the counter. Let him be the heartbroken, bereft one now. It was high time I put myself first.

I worked my shift with a stubborn determination, refusing to glance at the table he occupied, feeling a mixture of relief and vindication when Jennifer pointed to his retreating form as he finally left the cafe.

"Do you think he's out of his mind?" Stevie whispered, sounding amused, as she wiped down the espresso machine while we closed up for the night. "Spewing nonsense about coming from some other place? What is he, like an alien or something?" she laughed.

"Girl, I wish I knew," I responded. "Why would he make up such a far-fetched lie anyway? Like, if you're gonna lie to win someone back, make it believable at least, you know? It's the lack of effort for me."

"No wonder you said he was so good in bed," said Stevie, shaking her head. "It's always the crazy ones with the best D." I just rolled my eyes. "So, you're done with him for good then?" Stevie probed, looking at me intently with concern in her hazel eyes.

I stared back at her in sheer disbelief at her question. "Are you kidding me? He basically told whoever was on the phone that I was easy!"

"Well, you did sleep with him on the first date," Stevie couldn't hold back another giggle, which earned her a dish towel tossed in her direction.

"And your little black book could make a frat boy blush, but I'd never gossip like that about you," I countered.

"Okay, that's a bit of an exaggeration, but I get it, you're upset, so I'll gonna let it slide," she said rationally. When Stevie realized I was sulking and dejected, her tone softened. "I know you're not like that, Erica. Anyone who knows and respects you knows how you are."

"Exactly. Any guy who would say such awful things doesn't respect me," I concluded. "This whole situation just gave me huge red flags, Stevie," I said as I focused on cleaning up.

Stevie was silent for a moment. "He did seem to really regret it in the end, Erica. Plus, the guy's loaded. Just saying. Maybe string him along for some gifts, fancy meals, and some good dick every now and then?" Her words hung between us, unanswered.

If I ignored this glaringly obvious warning and things got worse afterward, the only person at fault would be me. I couldn't do it. And yet, I couldn't believe that just the night before, I was considering something real with this guy. I almost felt like dating again thanks to him. I had even asked him to decorate a Christmas tree together.

Something I only did with my family! I cringed at my own naivety. For all I knew, this begging-for-forgiveness act was just another game to Devin that he would laugh at me about later with his phone buddy. I felt stupid enough. I didn't want it to happen again.

"Stevie, no. I think I'd prefer to just end it. I'd rather stay single than get wrapped up in a toxic relationship."

Stevie placed a hand on my shoulder in a comforting gesture. "Couldn't be me. I would have dog-walked him. Took him for all he's worth. But, we're different that way. I understand."

Devin

I stood in the kitchen, seasoning the sauce for a simple dish of shrimp and lobster fettuccine alfredo. It was a meal I had come to enjoy in the human lands. Italian food, in general, was pleasant to me, and ironically enough, I was always mistaken for Italian upon dining at their restaurants. It was amusing, to say the least. I guess some of my people shared similar features to theirs when in our human forms.

I chewed my bottom lip, my shoulders tensing in frustration. Eating a dinner that I enjoyed tonight was supposed to be a decent pick-me-up, but my mind refused to stop replaying what happened today. It was torturous. Erica had been so upset with me. And here I thought I could just explain everything to Erica. I thought I could simply tell her the truth, and she'd forgive me.

What the hell was I thinking? Why did I think that would work? If anything, the truth has made things worse! Now, she wanted nothing to do with me. I've never seen her look at me that way before. "It's really over, huh?" I said out loud to no one.

Think! I commanded myself internally as I stirred the sauce pot aggressively. *How do I get her back?*

A cold and calculating but rational thought crossed my mind.

It wasn't Erica, necessarily, who I needed. I could target someone else. My looks have taken me far in this land. I could find another woman to fall for me. Hell, even a man if I grew desperate enough. Technically, anyone who meets the criteria could be used to lift the curse. There are billions of people on the planet...

But that thought was gone as quickly as it arrived - I knew I wanted Erica. After our time together, there was no going back. It was the way she laughed, the honesty in her eyes, the purity of her heart, her beauty, the way she spoke about the people and things she loved. *Fuck.*

It hit me quickly and painfully. I could barely understand or believe it, but I was falling for this little human woman.

This was not part of the plan. I wanted to slap myself. No wonder the strange, dull ache in my chest had begun to grow the longer I spent away from her. This realization made things so much worse. I would have to tell her the whole truth now. There was no other way.

CHAPTER SIX

Erica

I stumbled into my apartment late, peeling off the day's clothes and diving into pajamas with a speed born of pure need to shed the day off my skin.

Luna circled my legs, meowing softly.

"Poor girl," I chided, scratching her behind her ear. "Mommy's thoughts have been all over the place lately. You must be lonely."

She meowed in response as if to confirm this, and I felt my heart sink a little.

"Come, let's get you some food." I refilled her food and water bowls and watched my distractingly cute furbaby eat. She didn't eat much and soon walked over to her beloved feather teaser toy. I took the hint and engaged her immediately, grabbing the stick end and waving the feather above her head and all around her, watching her give chase and swipe at the toy as if it were prey.

I laughed happily at her silliness, but I could only distract my racing mind for so long. As if possessed, I reached for my phone, my fingers itching to dial Johnathan's number. I suddenly missed him badly. And the worst part was that I knew just how crazy that sounded. It filled me with shame.

How desperate and pathetic would it look to call him now? What exactly would I even say? That I had been with someone else who screwed me over and now I missed him? Ridiculous. He and Magda would surely have a nice long laugh at that from their hotel in Tulum. Besides, I knew I didn't truly miss him. I missed being in love. I missed feeling loved. I didn't miss the lying, selfishness, or the cheating. Absolutely not.

Memories from the previous night swarmed me as I closed my eyes. Devin's hands on my body as he drew me closer in bed, his chest pressed into my back as he fucked me in the shower, his voice ragged with desire, whispering in my ear...

A knock at the door yanked me from my thoughts. I made my way to the door while wondering who could possibly be knocking at this late hour.

"Erica, it's me," I heard Devin's voice from the other side. "You don't have to open the door,' he continued. "Just look through the peephole. There's something you need to see."

I didn't ponder how Devin knew where I lived. Instead, I found myself at the door, having turned on the outdoor light to see him properly as I peered through the viewer. The fisheye lens distorted his figure slightly, and but, what I could make out of him seemed downright impossible. Devin's skin had taken on a strange, light, silvery-gray pallor. Compelled by a mixture of fear and fascination, I flung the door open.

There, where Devin had just been standing, was a statue, an exact replica of him ... if he was a creature with massive, folded wings, fangs, and clawed hands. It was stunning and horrifying all at once.

What. The. Actual. Hell.

My hand reached out, almost of its own accord, and touched the stone surface of Statue Devin's outstretched hand, running my hands over the sharp nails. It was cold, immovable — real stone.

Then, shockingly, his eyes glowed bright and his stone hand began to move, wrapping around mine. Panic surged through me as I tried to withdraw, but his grip was un-yielding. Slowly, warmth returned to the stone, and before my eyes, the rock crumbled away from him like grains of silver sand, vanishing as they hit the ground. His wings had disappeared, as had his fangs and claws. The ashen exterior of his skin had melted away too, revealing his usual olive-toned complexion.

Devin stood before me again, brushing shimmering silver dust from his hair and looking as confused as I felt.

"How did you do that?" he asked, shaking his head as if to clear it.

"What the hell did you just — ? How were you just a winged rock monster just now?!" I screamed, my voice a mixture of sheer horror and disbelief as I stumbled back. My heart pounded violently against my ribcage, my brain refusing to acknowledge that I had just witnessed a man transform from a stone creature to flesh.

Devin lifted a finger to my lips and looked around as though fearful someone had overheard me.

"Can I come in?" he asked, urgency clear in his tone. At my skeptical stare, he added, "I'll explain everything. No more secrets." He looked mentally sound and level-headed, even given these crazy circumstances. I relented and stood aside to let him in before closing the door.

Upon removing his shoes, he followed me to the kitchen, sitting at the round wooden table next to me.

"What did I just witness?" I asked him flatly. I looked Devin up and down, trying to contain my fear. "What - what the hell are you?"

He ran a hand through his tousled dark curls, and licked his lips apprehensively before responding, "A gargoyle shifter."

I stared, dumbfounded. "A ... gargoyle ... shifter?" I repeated, bewildered. "Gargoyle ... like the kind that flies and guards buildings? Like the cartoon?"

A smile tugged at Devin's lips. "Not exactly. Though, in my land, we occasionally guard resources as decided upon by the royal family."

"What land is that?" I asked him. "Hell, what country is that? You've *never* even told me where you're from." I figured I might as well hear it all.

"I come from another realm, in a land they call Gorantha. It's similar to the human lands of Earth in many ways, but also very different."

"Different, how?"

"One one our years are longer than your. There's more oxygen in our atmosphere, so things are bigger there. Bigger animals, bigger trees, bigger produce."

Bigger dicks. I was glad I didn't say this out loud. Instead, I said, "So what are you doing all the way out here, in the human lands of the Earth realm, Gargoyle Devin?" I asked him, trying and failing to sound casual. "This is ... pretty unreal," I admitted.

"I know," Devin sighed quietly. "As for why I'm here, well, I can't exactly return home. Aranthena, the woman with power and influence I mentioned earlier, banished me from my homeland. She's a member of the royal family — an heiress and the future queen. She's reckless and impulsive, but her status grants her immeasurable authority. My family holds a high rank where I'm from, but we're still under the royal family's rule. I bruised the heiress' ego when I turned down her romantic advances once, so ... she punished me with banishment to 'humble me.' It's considered taboo to fraternize with someone who has been exiled by a member of the royal family. They might take it as a slight against them. So, I've avoided most of my family and friends ever since. ...In the end I chose to prioritize protecting my loved ones over the pain of my seclusion."

I could tell by the unconcealed pain in his eyes that he was being sincere. In the time that I had known him, I had never seen him look so downhearted. "I remember you were telling me how she cursed you," I started carefully, feeling embarrassed at how I'd reacted to him when he first brought it up. "Did the heiress punish you by making it so you could turn to stone like you did just now?" I ventured.

"Not quite. See, gargoyle shifters can naturally change from creature to human and from stone to flesh at will. But the heiress' curse makes it so that I'm turning to stone against my will. It's a gradual process, but eventually, I'll remain that way forever."

"And how-how do you break that curse? Can it be broken? Was that the task you mentioned before?" I pressed.

"Yes. According to the stipulations of the curse, the only way to lift it is if a pure-hearted person falls in love with me." Devin paused, and his eyes darted away from me as a bitter look came over his features. He swallowed thickly. "I can't help but think she banished me to Earth to make things more difficult for me. Not only is time faster here, but she knew the truth of who I am would create a barrier, preventing any human from truly loving me. She set me up to fail. My time is running short, and I'm finding it more difficult to maintain this human form each day. Still, I have to break it somehow and return home."

I listened this time without passing harsh and imme-diate judgment on Devin. Learning these new details of his situation affected me more than I was prepared for. What was happening to him and his family was all sorts of wrong. It was, frankly, tragic.

"I apologize," he spoke suddenly. "I didn't mean to dump this on you."

I ignored the comment. "How much time do you have?" was all I could think to ask.

"Months," he replied with an uneasy smile.

I shook my head, frustrated and confused. "If you manage to break free of your curse, why would you even want to go back?! After everything she's done to you? Couldn't she just get mad at you in the future and curse you again if she wanted?"

"I've considered that, yes," said Devin, "but my family needs me. I have to make sure they're all right. I can't let Aranthena take what our parents left for us. Not only is it unfair to punish my family because she's angry with me, it isn't even legal. ... But no one's stopping her," he clenched his fists tightly, his knuckles turning white. "So, I have to play her game for now. Beat her curse and hope it's enough to stop her. It's been unbearable trying to hold it together for my siblings' sake, despite not knowing if things will pan out. I'm sorry, Erica." His voice broke at the apology. "You didn't deserve to get hurt because of me."

I leaned back in my chair, weighing his words. "Why are you risking so much to tell me all this?" I asked finally. "I could expose you publicly, tell people what you are. Have you put in a museum, a science lab, or a freak show. ...Maybe set you up in someone's front yard."

Devin scoffed lightly at my digs. "First of all," he started, sounding a little offended and a little amused, "no one could contain me to a museum, a freak show, or a front yard. I have means of preventing that. But, I'm risking a lot to tell you this because," he reached out and gently caressed my cheek with the back of his hand, " ... I think I'm starting to fall for you."

I resisted the urge to lean into his touch and instead backed away a bit.

At any other time, that confession would have at least flattered me, but under these circumstances, they only served to irk me. "Devin, are you hearing yourself? You just admitted to planning some elaborate scheme to make me love you all so you can go 'home.' How do you expect me to believe you aren't trying to manipulate me right now?" I threw my hands up in exasperation. "And I'm still trying to wrap my head around the existence of different realms, and humans who can transform into damn stone monsters!"

"*Gargoyles.*"

"Whatever!"

"It's a lot. I get it," he agreed, his voice infuriatingly calm, as though he were the rational one. "It's part of the reason I decided to just show you my stone-state. Figured it would be easier than trying to explain it." He lifted his hand, and sharp, black, three-inch claws protracted from his fingertips, much like Luna's. I gasped and flinched back. He retracted them with a look of guilt for having startled me. "Look, Ri. This is hard on me, too. I didn't expect to feel this way."

"This is too much," I said earnestly, rising to my feet. "You-you have to go. I need some space to think."

"Y-yeah," he agreed, looking as if he had not expected things to go this way at all. "Of course." I was relieved when he rose to his feet and didn't argue. I followed him to the door. Neither of us could look at each other, the air was thick with tension. Devin gave my shoulder a gentle squeeze, before leaving quietly.

When he was gone, I locked the door behind him and yanked the curtains closed. Luna reentered the kitchen tentatively. I scooped her up in my arms and paced my kitchen, the reality of what had just unfolded seemed even more bizarre. A freaking gargoyle? He came from somewhere called Gorantha, which definitely wasn't on Earth. And, he was some cursed, high-ranking exile? It felt like something straight out of a fantasy novel.

My mind kept replaying the memory of him as a solid stone statue, the eerie sensation of his skin shifting from cold stone to warm flesh beneath my touch. It was a sensation that I could compare to nothing else. It was completely and undeniably otherworldly. The realization that

Gargoyles were not just a myth and other worlds existed beyond Earth, hit me like a wave. Yet, it was Devin's words about me that shook me the most.

He was falling in love with me? That was absurd. We'd only been on one date. Sure, the sex was incredible, and our conversations had been enjoyable, even captivating at times, but it was all moving too fast.

I considered calling Stevie but promptly changed my mind. This was too much to dump on her without sounding unhinged. Maybe a shower would help clear my thoughts. I got up and headed to the bathroom.

I slipped a shower cap over my hair and then stepped under the warm shower spray. As I felt the water running down my body, I was determined to wash away the chaos of Devin's visit. Nothing made sense anymore; it felt like the boundaries between truth and lies had entirely blurred.

Devin

My hands trembled as I carefully pulled out the scrying bowl, my shoulders tense with anxiety. Like an apparition turned to flesh, my younger brother, Duran, appeared in the bowl, watching me, his eyes glowing in the shadows of his hood.

"Brother," he whispered, "is everything all right?" his voice carried slightly, and it was clear he was speaking to me from a small, dark room like a closet.

I took a deep breath. "It will be, but Duran, I can't go home just yet," I confessed. Duran removed his hood and moved closer to his own scrying bowl as if to see my face better. His cherub face paled at the sight of me.

"You're turning," he spoke softly. "The curse ... it's taken hold of you..."

I smiled, trying to mask the pain in my chest as my heart ached to be near Erica. "It hasn't got me completely. Not entirely. Not yet. I've found my mate, brother. I still need her to accept me. But if she does, this retched curse will be lifted for good, and the heiress will have no grounds to take our home. You and Danae be all right again."

"I understand. I'll care for things for now. Don't worry. Focus on you," Duran said with a maturity that impressed me. I was proud of him and told him so before we hung up. I returned the bowl to its place in the cabinet and shut the door before sitting back on my heels and running my hands through my hair, and down the side of my cheek and jaw. Pieces of silver grains of stone fell to my lap at the action.

Realistically, what were the chances of Erica loving me? I questioned myself. I had already offended her. There was no doubt she saw me as a strange creature to fear and avoid at all costs. And then there was my little brother Duran and my precious sister, Danae. ... If I failed to lift the curse, their sorrow and pain would weigh on me forever. I couldn't imagine my siblings being homeless, not when I had told my parents that I would shoulder the responsibility of protecting our family before they passed.

I shuddered at the thought of approaching the heiress, begging her to release the curse, begging her to accept me as a companion after all. One of many, no doubt. ...No! I shut down the thought almost as soon as it came to me. She was too proud to take back someone who had rejected her, and I was too proud to take such a ruthless woman as my partner.

I wanted Erica, and that was all. I would have her and her alone, one way or the next.

Chapter Seven

E rica

The days drifted into an aching, empty monotony after my encounter with Devin when he showed up in a monstrous form at my doorstep, with skin cold, hard and gray as granite. Each day that I worked, I half-expected him to show up at the cafe again. The anticipation of his presence hung in the air like a heavy fog, dense and consuming. Yet, his absence was even more pronounced, an unsung melody that lingered just beyond the reach of my senses. Part of me wondered if I'd ever see him again. When Stevie, and even Jennifer, asked about him, I could only shrug.

As I drove into the dimly lit parking lot of the coffee shop on Christmas Eve, the reality of the holiday struck me with a sudden pang. The world was draped in festive lights, and merry music played all over the radio and at every mall, yet inside my chest, there was a hollow space where the cheer failed to penetrate. I realized I'd be alone for Christmas. I swallowed back the urge to cry.

Impulsively, I thought back to my parents, but I didn't want to worry them with my sorrows. Instead, I pulled out my phone and Face-Timed my older sister, Tracey, seeking the comfort of her familiar smile. Her face, illuminated by the soft glow of her phone, was a reminder of home — a home I was too far from this year.

"Erica! How are you?" she asked. Her voice was a lullaby of normalcy, the chaos of her household a stark contrast to my silent apartment. She looked radiant in her white wool sweater, her silk-pressed tresses fell to her shoulders in waves, an, she wore festive red lipstick and a beautiful smile.

"I'm okay," I replied, the words a half-truth that tasted bittersweet on my tongue. "Just feeling the distance today." I felt tears well up in my eyes, but I willed them away.

"Mommy? Cookies?" I could hear my baby niece, Isabelle, in the distance.

"After dinner," Tracey told her daughter. I could sense her maternal warmth even despite our distance. She turned back to me. "It's such a shame we can't all be with you this year. But you're in our hearts, Ri. We'll make plans to visit in the New Year."

"Yes, all right."

"So, how's your love life these days? I always say that when someone walks out of your life, don't get upset. Be grateful, because they're making room for someone better." I knew she was talking about Johnathan because I had never told her about Devin.

Still, when she inquired about my recent love life, I felt the edges of my reality blur. I confessed to a date with Devin and pointed out his positive traits, leaving out the part where the man was not entirely ... human. How could I explain Devin's truth? That he was more a creature of stone and spell, an enigma wrapped in the night? I couldn't, and so I didn't.

"Men are stupid creatures sometimes," said Tracey. "They often make mistakes as you know."

"I do!" I agreed.

"*But*," she continued as though I had not interrupted her. "The good ones will own up to their ,mistakes and do better. Your face lit up when you spoke of this Devin guy just now. It's the holidays, give him a chance. Besides, Erica, you owe it to yourself to be happy," she encouraged. Tracey's advice cut short by the demands of her teeming household. "Love you, sis."

"You too," I replied.

Her words echoed in my mind as I stepped inside the cafe, a sanctuary of scents - baked goods, teas, and coffees, and of comfort. And there he was — Devin — seated in the corner, looking every bit the haunted figure from a gothic romance. Dressed in a long black overcoat, his slightly damp curls hung heavy over his face, partially covering his eyes; silent and captivating, he nursed a coffee and stared at the falling snow through the window.

"Hey," I managed, my voice a tremulous note that belied the chaos of my racing thoughts.

His steel-gray eyes shifted to me, his handsome face etched with the marks of a struggle only he could understand, the physical toll of his otherworldly existence.

"You came," he observed, his voice a silken thread pulling at the knots in my soul.

"Well, I do work here," I quipped, a weak attempt at humor to shield my suddenly vulnerable heart.

"Fair point," Devin smiled.

I let out a breath I didn't know I was holding and smiled back. I missed his smile, I realized.

I pulled out the chair across from him and sat down. My shift wouldn't start for another half-hour.

"Are you okay?" I asked him, instantly fearing it was a stupid question. Clearly, he'd seen better days. He looked so tired.

"I am now," he professed. "I'm just happy to see you. To be near you." There was a reverence in his tone that warmed me. I reached out and touched his hand. Instantly, I watched color flood his cheeks and lips, and what I realized was stone dust, and not snow, disappeared from his hair.

"Whoa," I remarked, pulling back in awe.

"You make me feel alive, princess," he said, winking. I looked down, embarrassed suddenly by that nickname. He'd used it a lot that one night that we were intimate. That night replayed in my mind more than I cared to admit.

"Mind if I keep you company during your shift?" he asked, tearing me out of my intrusive thoughts.

"Stay. I don't mind," I said earnestly.

We conversed in the stolen moments during my shift when I wasn't busy. And amusingly enough, it was Jennifer who seemed a little annoyed with me for once. ("Erica, a customer is waiting! *Jesus*, I never get any help around here.")

Devin asked me about my family, and I told him how my mother had moved to the States in her teens and met my father in college. How my sister had birthed my niece only three years ago. How excited I was to be an auntie, and my whole family's plans to spend time together with me in the New Year. I asked to hear more about his world, and Devin's tales of Gorantha enveloped me in a mixture of fantasy and longing. He told me of the winter traditions in that realm, how they would make a stone circle on the solstice to welcome back the sun. The normalcy of his company disguised the extraordinary nature of his being.

After work, as he walked me to my car, the world around us seemed to quiet, to still, until there was only Devin and I. I leaned in and embraced him, his warmth shielding me against the cold night air.

"Thanks for keeping me company tonight," I spoke against his chest. I felt tears sting my eyes, not for the first time today.

He squeezed me tight. "It's all right." A moment passed before he said, "Listen, I don't expect you to trust me again soon. But, I wanted to let you know things have changed for me. It seems I won't be leaving the human lands as originally planned."

"You're staying?" I asked him directly.

"I am."

"Just like that, huh?" I searched his eyes for a hint of deception but found none.

Aware that I doubted his confession, Devin said, "I'm telling you this because I wondered if you could find it in your heart for us to start again? I don't want to use you to lift my curse or to fulfill my desires. I simply, honestly, want us to get to know each other. I want to make memories with you. To partake in your traditions and form new ones ... if you want that too."

His plea for a new beginning, to know and be known without the shadows of his past, reached out to me, an offering laid bare. The idea of second chances, of trust after deceit, was a fragile thing, a newly formed ice over a deep lake. I pulled away from him enough to study his features, searing this version of him into my mind.

"I'd like that," I told him honestly. I'd missed him so much. "... If you mean it."

"I'm here," he assured me. "I'm not going anywhere."

Those words should have felt like an anchor, yet they floated around me like snowflakes, unique and transient. Time would tell.

"Merry Christmast," he said with a hopeful smile, his mistake a shard of innocence in the complex mosaic of who he was.

"It's Christmas," I corrected him with a gentle laugh, a sound that seemed too light for the gravity of the moment. "And same to you."

Erica

The solitude of my bed that night was a stark contrast to the evening's revelations. Thoughts of Johnathan, and our past wove through my mind, but their sting had lessened with time. And there was Devin, his presence a new variable, an unknown in the equation of my life.

I still couldn't believe he had chosen to stay, to be a part of this world, of my world. The warmth of his words lingered, a subtle heat that coaxed a hesitant bloom of hope in my chest.

I want it to be true...

On Christmas Eve, as the rest of the world celebrated in a symphony of joy and togetherness, I lay alone, contemplating the web of possibilities that Devin's stay might weave. And in that quiet, still night, I allowed myself the luxury of not deciding — of simply being. There was still time for my love story to unfold and for me and Devin, perhaps, to be rewritten under the tender gaze of the snow-strewn sky.

Devin

Even though I lay in bed, my mind raced a mile a minute. I couldn't help it. The gargoyle's curse still coursed within me, a beast tamed by the gentle touch of Erica's hand.

Erica. She drifted through my thoughts like a melody, the embodiment of all that was good, light, and pure. All that I yearned to hold onto – like my own humanity. In her eyes, I saw the reflection of a man, not a creature of myth, and it was that man who needed to earn her trust, her smile, and her laughter again.

I made a silent vow then: Enough talk. I would show Erica that she had my heart. I would be the steadfast presence at her side. I would be there, at her side always, so she never walked alone. I would show her just how steady and firm I could be. She didn't hate me. She wanted me still. And so I knew things would be okay and my curse would break in due time, but I would never give her reason to distrust me again.

In such a short time, I'd learned so much about humanity, of its frailties, and its immense capacity for love. I came to understand that love was an act of constant becoming. So, I would become. For her, I would transform every day. And as my heart began to shift from granite to something far more vulnerable, I'd hold onto the hope that the steady beat of this new, flesh-bound heart resonated with hers.

Erica was my mate. In her hands, I'd place my existence. And, I was hers, in every sense. I would love her forever. Whether she decided to be mine, to bind her life with a creature of dusk and dawn, remained unknown. But that is the nature of true love — it asked for nothing, yet offered everything.

She had my heart, and in time, I hoped to have hers. For now, I would wait, I would hope, and I would love.

CHAPTER EIGHT

Devin

I awoke just minutes before dawn to find my room engulfed by a strange purple glow that emanated from beneath my bedroom door. Suddenly alert, I rose from my bed, my gargoyle fangs instinctively dropping into place as my body's fight or flight mechanism activated. Slowly, I turned the doorknob, and stepped out into the hallway, following the eerie light to the cabinet in my living room. I realized it was my scrying bowl before I even opened it.

It usually glows white, I mused.

Nonetheless, I realized I was receiving a phone call from my realm. Sitting down in front of my cabinet, I swung open its doors, picked up the bowl and held it in my lap. My mind ran on Duran and Danae, my siblings. I prayed they were all right. Taking a deep breath, I accepted their phone call.

The fogginess of the bowl cleared slowly and gave way to a figure. Startled, I jumped back with a shout, nearly dropping my communication device when I took sight of the person staring at me from the other end of the bowl. It was the heiress herself - Aranthena.

"What the hell?!" I blurted out.

"Good to see you too, Devin," she said, her tone deceptively innocent. Though I had not seen her in nearly two years, time had been kind to her. She'd barely aged since the day she had ordered my banishment. Her long auburn hair was still pinned up in its signature chignon bun with a flower beret, and she wore one of her iconic green bardot dresses that complimented her deeply tanned skin. She had always been considered pretty back home, in a very plain, conventional way. And as things stood, she was easily the last person, in all the realms, whom I wanted to see.

"Why did you call me?" I snapped. A haunting thought occurred to me. "What have you done to my family?!"

"Relax," she spoke calmly. "I've done nothing. They're unharmed."

"And what of our home, and family assets?" I gritted my teeth, irritated, my fangs on full display. It wasn't respectful to bear one's teeth at a member of the royal family, but I thought: *So what? What would she do next, exile me to hell?* Surprisingly, Aranthena simply closed her eyes and shook her head, reminiscent of how a teacher might respond to a petulant child.

"I just called to inform you that I've called off the seizure of your family's home and assets. I have no interest in them anymore."

"Yeah? Why the change of heart?" I asked, skeptically.

She seemed to fight the urge to lash out at me, I could see her annoyance pull her lips taut. She took a breath. "Well, Devin, after some thought, I realized it was a little petty to punish your family over a personal gripe I had with you, is all. Besides, when I become the future queen, I need to display a certain level of ... how did my mentor put it again ... ah, yes, temperance."

My fangs slid back into my jaws as I felt myself calm a bit. Still, I did not want to let my guard down completely. She was known to play games, to tell half-truths, while smiling in your face.

"I paid your siblings a visit the other day," she continued. "Your brother, Duran, tells me you've found your fated mate in a human woman. Is that right?"

I hesitated to respond to her words. What if I confirmed them and she targeted Erica? It was too risky.

"Your silence speaks volumes," she assured me after a moment of palpable pause. "Look," she started. "I won't interfere in your life anymore. You've found something sacred, something that's stronger than baneful magic ... if you can make it work, that is."

Although I appreciated the idea of my family finally being left alone, I couldn't shake my confusion. "Why are you telling me all this?"

"Because ... you've always cherished deep connections, and I realize now that it's something I also desire. I no longer want to be accessible to just any guy I fancy or whoever finds me pretty. All the men I've engaged with have been unserious, and eager for any woman's attention. All except for you. You've always only had eyes for your mate, even when you didn't know her, couldn't see her. You waited for her. I want that. I want someone who only wants me too."

I nodded in understanding, feeling my compassion toward her growing. "Everyone deserves a love like that," I agreed in a softer tone, "if they want it."

"That's all I'll accept from now on."

"You're worthy," I assured her. "You'll find it."

Her amber eyes glistened with unshed tears, and she dropped her gaze. "Yes," she agreed. "I know." When she looked at me again, she was smiling.

We ended the call and I sat with the scrying bowl in my hands for another few minutes, in silent reflection.

I'd never seen that side of the heiress before. That humbleness or calm. I could only wish her well and gave thanks to the gods that my family would be okay. The curse was still upon me, but for once I could feel its hold loosening. Eventually, it would break. I was certain of it.

Erica

I chose to let the steady tick of time measure the trust I was slowly rebuilding in Devin. It wasn't just his promises that needed to hold weight—it was the consistency of his actions. And like clockwork, Devin was there, a constant through the flux of days. He'd arrive just before closing time to keep me company and walk me to my car. His presence was a silent vow of commitment as he escorted me to my car under the winter night sky.

On the cusp of the New Year, with the world holding its breath for fresh beginnings, I found myself gazing up into Devin's eyes. There was an undeniable pull, a need that was both new and as old as time itself. I wanted the new year to start with his kiss, a seal on the promises we hadn't yet made aloud.

He had taken me out for dessert and drinks, and we were standing next to his car in the parking lot, much like the first time at the restaurant.

"I want you to kiss me," I whispered, our hands intertwined as if they were the roots of what we could become.

He grabbed the back of my neck and gently pressed his warm, full lips to mine. Our lips met in a kiss that was a revelation. A gasp escaped me—not from surprise, but from the visceral reaction that unfurled within me. It was a warmth, a pull in my chest that tethered me to him in a way I couldn't explain. The sensation was bewildering, yet I clung to it, to him, wrapping my arms around him in a silent plea for more.

"I'm not going anywhere, Erica," he breathed into my ear, the chuckle in his voice sending a shiver down my spine.

His words were like a harmony to the thrumming in my heart, a rhythm that quickened at his proximity.

"What's this feeling?" I had to ask; a part of me fearing some sort of enchanting gargoyle magic was at play.

"What do you mean?" His question came as he captured my hands in his, grounding me as if he could steady the fluttering in my chest.

"This... intensity when we kissed. This thrumming inside me." The words tumbled out, unfiltered and raw.

His expression shifted then, the levity fading into an earnestness that stilled the night air. He didn't dismiss my concerns with a laugh or a quip. Instead, he looked utterly taken aback, yet there was no confusion in his gaze, only a dawning realization.

"What?" My voice rose, tinged with an urgency I couldn't mask. What was he not telling me?

"I didn't think..." He paused as if struggling with the weight of his words. "Erica, there's something I need to explain to you. Let's go somewhere private." The cold seemed to press in on us as we stood outside the restaurant, the festive air now charged with a tension that begged for resolution.

"Sure. We can go to my place." My agreement was swift, propelled by a desire for answers and a fear of what those answers might be. The unknown thrumming in my chest was now matched by the beating of my heart, racing towards a future unknown.

We drove through the streets, the hum of the car's engine beneath us. In the quiet, charged space between us, my hand reached out for his. He gave me a reassuring squeeze and a quick smile before turning his attention back to the road. The moment our skin connected, that sweet, aching thrum returned to my chest as a pleasant sensation spread throughout my body, as shocking as it was beautiful.

Stepping into the warmth of my place, we unwrapped ourselves from the cold, removing our boots and coats. I headed towards the living room, but I soon noticed a pause in Devin's footsteps as he stood frozen at the room's threshold. I eyed him quizzically before following his gaze and realizing what had caught his attention.

My Christmas tree stood proudly by the fireplace, its brilliant, multicolored lights flashing rhythmically in a mesmerizing glow that lit up the room.

"You ... like it?" I asked, feeling a little awkward suddenly.

Devin's eyes shifted towards me; they were soft. "You did a wonderful job," he said sweetly. He walked over and touched a round ornament as though he'd never seen one before.

I made my way next to him, peering at the red and gold ornament that had caught his attention. Instantly, I recognized the ornament ball in his grip. "My grandmother gave me that one when I was nine. I've kept it ever since," I shared. "It has a special place in my heart even more now that she's passed. She even crafted it herself."

"It's truly lovely," Devin said with admiration. He looked at me with a smile, and I returned it, but beneath both our smiles was a little sadness. We were supposed to decorate a tree together last year. Yet our falling out caused us to miss that chance.

He tucked a braid behind my ear with such tenderness that my breath hitched.

"I'll make sure to add an ornament to your tree this year when we decorate," he promised. "Maybe dance and drink sorrel too."

I couldn't contain my joy as I beamed up at him. "Yes! I look forward to it. I'll bake cookies." I touched his shoulder and felt that odd feeling in my chest again. I held a hand to my chest. "What is that?" I stared up at him expectantly. Devin took my hand and walked me to the sofa, where we sat down.

"Okay," Devin breathed deeply, studying me intently. "I didn't expect you to feel the bond so soon, Erica. Know that I'd wait centuries for you if I had to." The power in his words invaded my heart and held it hostage.

Butterflies fluttered frantically in my belly as I replied, "What bond? W-what're you talking about, Dev?" My spine straightened, and my hands moved to my hips instinctively.

He inhaled, trying again. "What I meant was that our souls recognize each other as companions from lifetimes before. Simply put, we're meant to be together as decided by fate."

Silence fell heavily around us as his words weighed on me. I had heard the term "soul mates" before. But I was never sure I believed in it, especially not after being betrayed by the man I thought I'd spend the rest of my life with.

"Is this … some kind of gargoyle magic, Devin? Did you do this to us somehow? Was this on purpose?" My voice came out much smaller than I intended.

"No!" he said sternly, shutting down my intrusive thoughts. "No. I swear to you, I had no hand in this. Besides, that's completely impossible. There is no power great enough to imitate a mating bond. It is beyond our realms. It's sacred. …And honestly, not everyone meets their mate in every lifetime. I was completely shocked when I felt it between us – " His words tumbled out, tripping over one another in their haste.

"How long have you known about this?" I pushed, feeling the frantic pulse of my heart again.

"Since you touched my hand and brought me back from stone in your at your doorsteps. That isn't normal, Erica. Only a mate can do that."

"So, that's why you're still here? Because I'm your mate?"

"Yes," he answered with raw honesty. "It tortures me to be away from you."

I studied his earnest face, feeling an irresistible pull toward him, toward the thrumming of our hearts. Yet, apprehension shadowed the edges of my desire.

"What if I refused to be mated to you? What if I wanted you to go away?"

He seemed to look right through me. "You don't," he said knowingly.

"But what if I did?" I insisted. I needed to know I had autonomy over myself.

His response was immediate and firm, though pain splintered through the stoic facade. "If you wanted me to go, then I'd leave and never bother you again, I swear it. I desire only to bring you happiness, protect, and provide for you. If you preferred I leave you in peace, I'd fight for a place in your heart. But ... if that failed, then I'd retreat into solitude away from you."

And I believed him. But it wasn't my mind that led me to trust him; it was my body, my soul. My arms found their way around his neck, his body almost trembling at my touch.

"What does this mean?" Devin murmured against my skin as I kissed his jaw and down his neck.

"Don't get any big ideas, soul mate," I teased, laughter bubbling through the intensity of the moment. "But you can stay the night."

He swept me up, my legs instinctively wrapping around his back, our heartbeats crescendoing together. His kisses were hungry yet restrained as if he were mindful of not pushing too far, too fast. In that carefulness, I found myself both grateful and burning with desire for him.

Pressing me up against the kitchen wall, his lips journeyed from my mouth down my neck, worshiping with every touch. I couldn't stifle the moan that rose from somewhere deep within me, every part of me vibrating with his touch.

There, in the kitchen, we made love with a slowness and an eagerness that was both a culmination and a promise, ending in echoes of pleasure on the tiled floor.

He took us to my bedroom, where we lay on my bed, listening to the wind howling outside my window. Distantly, I heard a meow and looked down to see Luna standing at the side of my bed.

I looked back at Devin to find him smiling fondly at her. "Bring her up here," he said simply, and so I scooped her up in my arms and sat her on the bed. Like a magnet, she wandered over to Devin nuzzled his chest.

"She's normally so standoffish, yet, for some reason she seems to like you a lot," I said shaking my head, equally amused and confused.

"She has good taste," Devin answered matter-of-factly, and scratched her just under her chin. She basked in the attention, purring happily before she got tired of us both and jumped down off the bed, walking out of the room.

"She rules this house," I explained to Devin light-heartedly. "I'm just lucky to be here."

He laughed at this. I propped up on my elbow and gazed down at the handsome man next to me. Devin was staring affectionately up at me with those jewel-like eyes, reaching out, he caressed my cheek with pure fondness.

"I don't know much about this gargoyle mate stuff, Devin," I told him earnestly. "But ... I'd like for you to stick around."

He took my wrist in his hand. "Well, good thing we've got a lot of time to figure it out," he said, lowering his mouth to my wrist. I jumped when I felt his fangs graze my skin as he grinned against it. "And, it would be my honor, princess," he said, planting a tender kiss.

And as we drifted into sleep, entwined in each other's embrace, our hearts found a synchrony, a silent acknowledgment of a bond that was, perhaps, destined.

THE END

CHAPTER NINE

Author's Note

Thank you so much for reading. Please be sure to leave a review if you enjoyed my work. As an indie author, with no real support systems outside of you beautiful readers, it definitely helps motivate me to keep going. I write to provide more relatable and diverse main characters in the romance book genres for you to root for and to see yourself in. I hope I was able to achieve that with this book and with books to come! Sending you all the joy and love in the world.

– Maddie Daniels